Tracy Tam: Santa Command

Krystalyn Drown

Published by Tantrum Books for Month9Books
Cover illustrated by Zach Schoenbaum
Cover and typography designed by Victoria Faye
Cover Copyright © 2014 Month9Books

For Kristi

Tracy Tam: Santa Command

Krystalyn Drown

CHAPTER ONE

Santa Command—Control Room 8
December 24th
2300 hours

The twenty-foot view screen was filled from corner to corner with one horrifying image: a brightly lit fireplace! A box popped up on a bottom corner of the screen, listing worst-case scenarios. It named everything from blistered feet to a flaming Santa.

Phil spoke frantically into his headset, sending Artie the order for an emergency Snow Drop. Artie, one of the techies on the lower level of the control room, grabbed his controller and began tapping buttons like he was fighting a boss on a video game. Except at Santa Command, there wasn't a restart button.

"This shouldn't have happened," Walt scolded. He reached in front of Phil and tapped out a string of commands on Phil's keyboard. The chances of Santa catching fire rose with each passing second. 23%. 48%. 76%.

Beads of sweat formed on Phil's forehead, but it was nothing compared to the heat he would feel if he messed this up. "Heat signs for the entire block were negative. I don't know how I missed it."

Walt folded his arms across his rather large stomach. He was like Santa's evil twin, making stops in each of Santa Command's control rooms whenever his beeper warned him of an emergency. Instead of bringing presents, he brought demotions and demerit points.

"How long?" he asked.

Phil spoke into his headset. "Rose Street Camera. Knot of Giant Oak. Pull back. Show me the sky."

A girl on the lower level punched a few buttons. The picture on the view screen rushed backwards, pulling away from the Tam's living room window and up into the star-filled sky. There was nothing else to see, not even the moon.

"Where is it, Artie?" Walt's normally rosy cheeks turned purple. The sleigh was on the roof. The big guy was two paces from the chimney.

"It's coming!" Artie shouted up to them.

"Not fast enough." Phil rubbed his temple. A headache was starting to form, and he couldn't think straight. He scanned the screen, back and forth, up and down.

Santa stood by the chimney with one foot raised in the air. His eyes were glazed over, oblivious to the smoke rushing out of the chimney.

"Come on. Come on. Come on!" Phil drummed his fingers on the desk. "There!" He pointed to the upper right corner of the screen. A tiny black dot had appeared, and it was quickly approaching.

"If he doesn't make it—" Walt warned.

"He'll make it. I'm not losing this Santa."

Phil held his breath as the black dot grew closer, revealing itself to be a large bird, not a real one, but close enough to fool the humans. There was a tan, leather bag clutched in its talons.

The man in the red suit lifted his leg over the chimney edge. The smoke touched the heel of his boot, then parted around it. The man didn't pause. He wasn't programmed to.

Phil buried his face in his hands. That type of mistake would certainly mean demotion and possibly the loss of his job.

Walt slammed his fist onto the control table. "Look!"

Phil's eyes popped back open. He caught his thumbnail between his teeth as Artie's remote control bird soared over the chimney top and dropped the white fluffy cargo down the hole, exactly one second before Santa hefted his other leg over, tossed a handful of yellow dust over his head, and dropped down the chimney.

"Rose Street Camera," Phil said in a nervous whisper, "show me the Tam living room."

The camera panned down to the window and showed Santa arranging presents around the twinkling tree. The fireplace was covered with a soft, white substance that would soon evaporate, leaving no trace it had ever existed.

Phil leaned back in his seat, running his hands back through his short, curly hair. He had saved his tail. This time.

He glanced at the calendar on the wall. Six months until he had enough money for his vacation. He'd been saving for years just so he could spend a month in Hawaii surfing, kayaking, and mountain climbing.

Walt's beeper went off again.

Of course. Phil sat back up. The relief never lasted long on December 24th.

Walt pointed to the bright red words that scrolled across the top of the screen. "Phil, we've got movement upstairs."

"Is it a parent?"

"Negative." Walt pressed a button, and several lines of green text appeared in a box at the top left corner of the screen.

Species: Human

Height: 4'9"

Age: 10

Speed: Slow

Destination: Appears to be the staircase

Phil smiled. This was why he'd been chosen to lead Control Room 8. He knew kids, and he knew how to distract them. He'd seen a lot in his years at Santa Command, and he'd once calculated that four out of ten children tried to catch a glimpse of Santa on Christmas Eve. Whether the kids sneaked out of bed, slept in the living room with one eye open, or hid in the chimney, he had a scenario for them all.

Phil spoke into his headset. "Rose Street Camera. Tam's Pine Tree. Give me the second story hallway."

One of the techies made the adjustment. The view screen switched from the living room to a dark hallway on the second floor.

"Night vision, please," Phil ordered.

The techie touched a key on his keyboard, and a night vision lens slid into place on the camera. The hallway was now lit in a green glow. Phil could clearly see Tracy Tam creeping past her parents' bedroom door. Her bare feet made no sound in the plush carpet, and she was careful to side step the jingly toys her kitten left scattered everywhere.

"Hm," Phil said. "Neatly brushed hair. No wrinkles

in her pajamas. She's been waiting up, most likely reading a book."

"Seems pretty routine."

"Affirmative." Phil called up another camera, asking for the new shot to be displayed as a smaller video in the corner of the screen. The hallway was still the main focus, but the corner screen showed the rooftop where eight tiny reindeer stood eerily still. He flipped a switch on his headset and transmitted a message to the ear buds worn by each reindeer. "Time to change."

Even though Phil had seen the transformation thousands of times, his mouth still dropped open in amazement. He knew enough about cameras and technology to create the appearance of magic, but these guys had the real thing. In less than an eye blink, the deer had shrunk out of their harnesses and morphed into their true forms—Inklings. About six inches tall with sharp brown features that made them look like they'd been carved from a tree, they were what most people mistook for elves. But they were so much more than that.

Sasha's squeaky voice chirped into Phil's headset. "Tell me this is gonna be fun."

Phil suppressed a laugh. The Inklings were tricky little buggers and cherished the one night of the year when their magic wasn't restricted to sneaking around as birds and squirrels, taking notes for the naughty and nice list. If they were judging themselves, they would make the naughty list every time.

"How about Diversion Scenario #3?" Phil suggested. Code Name: Wake up Mom.

Sasha cackled into the headset. As the tiny creatures dropped down the chimney and into the living room, Phil had the cameramen follow them so he wouldn't miss out on any of the fun.

Sasha started small. She and her team raced up the stairs, pausing at the very top. She motioned for the rest of them to stay back while she slunk into one of the shadows to retrieve a purple cat toy. It looked about the size of a bowling ball in her arms, and that was exactly how she used it. With perfect timing, she rolled it under Tracy's heel just as the girl passed her parents' bedroom. Tracy slipped and landed on her back with a soft thud.

"Oof!" she cried.

Her mother's sleepy voice drifted into the hallway. "Did you hear that?"

Tracy sat up straight and, with wide eyes, glanced back to her bedroom. It was only a few feet behind her.

That's right, thought Phil. *Go back to bed. There's nothing to see downstairs.*

Sasha's pointy face twisted into a frown. Many times, a small noise was all it took to send the kids scrambling back to bed.

"It's probably Santa." It was her father's voice this time. "He usually comes about now."

"Yeah," her mother said. "I bet you're right. I hope he brings that microscope Tracy's been asking for. I couldn't find it online."

"Mmm," her father said. "Go back to sleep. We'll see in the morning."

For a long moment, Tracy didn't move, but when no further sounds came from her parents' room, she stood up, brushed off her Superman pajamas, and resumed her creep toward the stairs.

"Uh oh," said Phil, even though he knew the first attempt only worked half the time. Quickly, he thought up another scenario. "Sasha, go for the snowflake."

Sasha nodded. She made a few hand motions to the seven Inklings behind her, and they moved into the hallway, arranging themselves in the Snowflake Position, each of them hidden in a dark corner of the hall. Time to amp up the game.

Tracy inched forward.

Sasha mumbled to the others. "Wait for it. Wait for it." Then, when Tracy stepped into the sweet spot, the center of the "snowflake," Sasha raised her hand into the air. The Inklings each pointed one finger toward Tracy and shot out a very low dose of magic, slightly chilled. To Tracy, it would have felt like the air conditioning flipped on and a breeze shivered across her skin. Cold, but not alarmingly so. Enough to send her scurrying for the warmth of her covers.

She lived in Florida, however, and the winter had been uncomfortably warm. When the air hit her, she smiled, welcoming the chill.

Walt's beeper squealed louder. "Fix this!" he demanded.

Tracy was inches from the stairway now, and once she got there, she'd be able to see straight down to the living room where Santa was filling her stocking. She crouched down as she got closer, and Phil caught a glimpse of his solution sitting in her shirt pocket. He relayed the information to Sasha.

As Phil's voice traveled through Sasha's tiny ear bud, Sasha saw exactly what Phil was referring to. That's why they worked as a team. Sasha saw the world from the ankles down. Phil and his cameras saw everything else. Sasha typed in a code to her wristcom and smiled as she sent out an activation signal to any wireless device within five feet. In this case, it was Tracy's cell phone, tucked carefully into her shirt pocket.

When the phone started blasting Beyoncé, Tracy yelped, then scrambled back to her bedroom. A split second later, her dad poked his head out of his room.

Mr. Tam looked up and down the hallway, but all he saw was Tracy's closed door and a bunch of shadows.

The Inklings were well hidden, camouflaged both by darkness and magic.

When he was satisfied his daughter was safely in bed, he went back into his room. His muffled voice carried into the hallway once more. "If she was on that phone again—"

"Don't," his wife said soothingly. "It's Christmas. She's probably gossiping with Kate, talking about what Santa will bring them."

"Fine," Mr. Tam sighed. "But next time, it's gone for a week."

As the house settled back into a peaceful slumber, Phil wiped the sweat off his forehead. "There. Crisis averted."

Walt raised one eyebrow. "Are you positive?"

"Well..." Phil surveyed the screen, which showed Santa still packing Tracy's stocking. Depending on how fast he worked, she had time to sneak out again. Phil ordered up another camera, this one in the bird's nest just outside Tracy's window. He had a clear shot of the curled up lump lying in her bed, and her long black hair trailing out from under the comforter and across her pillow. "Now, I'm positive."

"Good," Walt said. It was the closest to a compliment he ever gave on Christmas Eve. "Now, get Santa out of there and on to the next house."

Phil cracked his knuckles. "Bring it on."

CHAPTER TWO

Tracy

When Tracy's phone went off, she aborted Plan A and went straight to Plan B: Join the Party. She didn't like that she didn't get any video of Santa in her house, but she knew Plan B was where she would find the strongest evidence for her experiment.

She'd had her pillows and wig set up in her bed for hours, so it was a simple matter of climbing out of her window, which overlooked the roof. All she had to do was ease her way past her parents' window onto the larger section of roof over the garage. With no moon visible, she hoped it was dark enough that Santa and his elves wouldn't spot her. Did he bring his elves with him? She wasn't clear on the details, but that was where this experiment came in.

As she approached the sleigh, she noticed the absence of reindeer. Their reins were attached to the sleigh, sticking straight out, as if the animals were still in them, but they were nowhere in sight. She made a mental note: Reindeer = holograms? To her, that was more logical than the sign hanging on Santa's sleigh— Out for a drink of water. Be back in a flash.

Her grandmother always said that Santa's reindeer were glorious creatures, and that children should stay up at least once in their life to sneak a peek at them in flight. But Tracy knew that reindeer did not have wings, and without wings, they couldn't fly, plain and simple. Whatever her grandmother had seen had been an illusion.

Tracy circled the sleigh looking for a tiny projector or camera lens on the front of it to prove her theory. She couldn't find one, but at the back, she found something even better—a pair of jet engines attached between the sleigh's runners. *Yes!* Solid proof that the reindeer didn't actually fly the sleigh. By dawn, she was going to have a logical explanation for every aspect of Santa's big night.

She snapped several pictures with her phone, and then hopped into the back of the sleigh, breathing a sigh of relief that there weren't any elves hiding in there. After a quick glance around for Santa or nosy neighbors, she opened the notes file on her phone and added two words to the bottom—jet propulsion. Then, she slid her phone back into her pocket and burrowed beneath four giant red bags, settling in for a long night.

She had been preparing for this night for the past two and a half months, ever since she'd heard her mom talking on the phone to her Aunt Susan. Tracy only heard one side of the conversation, but it had been enough.

"That's wonderful, Suze!" her mom had said. "I can't believe you found a doctor that can help Pim!"

Tracy nearly screamed for joy when she heard that. Her cousin, Pim, had been her best friend before the accident. After Pim fell out of that tree, all she ever did was lie in bed and stare at the TV. Her doctors said she should be fine, but she wasn't. She couldn't walk, and she rarely spoke. Most of the time Pim wouldn't even blink to show she understood what people were saying to her. If her aunt had found a doctor who could help, that was the best news in the world.

Of course, it was followed by the worst news in the world.

"It's going to cost how much?" The sadness in her mother's voice made Tracy sick to her stomach. There was a doctor out there who could fix Pim, but her aunt couldn't afford him. "Oh honey, I'm so sorry. If we had that much, I'd give it to you in a heartbeat, but we just don't."

The words rung through Tracy's ears and bounced

around in her mind. It couldn't be the truth. After the phone call ended, Tracy marched straight up to her mom. "How could you tell her that? There's gotta be some way to get the money."

"Sweetheart, I know you miss having Pim around, but you have to understand that some things just aren't possible." Her mom reached out to tuck Tracy's hair behind her ear.

Tracy ducked out of the way. She was furious that her mom had done nothing. She hadn't talked to her dad about it. She hadn't asked her boss for a raise. She hadn't offered to take out a second mortgage on their house. In the movies, people did all of those things to come up with money when it was important.

Tracy folded her arms across her chest and leveled her eyes at her mom. It was a stare that often made her mom give in, or ground her, depending on the situation. "There is a way, and if you're not willing to find it, then I am."

The next week, her science teacher, Mr. Danner, gave her the answer on a bright green flyer.

"You should enter this," he said. "You're on the younger end, but I think you're smart enough to come away with at least an honorable mention prize."

"Prize?" Tracy's heart hammered wildly against her ribs as she traced the black lettering with her pointer finger.

State Science Fair

Open to all students Grades 5-8

Grand Prize: $5000

Tracy stopped reading there. Forget honorable mention, she was going for the grand prize. Five thousand dollars had to be enough to pay the doctor.

She spent the next few weeks combing the Internet and the library for ideas. It wasn't until she saw a magazine ad from the Santa Commission that she had her project. It reminded kids to have their lists in no later than November 20th so Santa's elves had time to organize. But still, it wasn't the reminder that gave her the idea—it was the slogan.

Even magic needs a helping hand.

Tracy had never believed in magic. Behind every famous magic act, there was a foundation of science. Simple physics did not allow one man to travel the world in one night, but somehow he did it. The Santa Commission's slogan became her hypothesis.

The first part of her plan was simple—wait upstairs until Santa arrived.

She went to bed like normal, but she wore a pouch around her neck that contained all of the necessary supplies: bags for collecting samples, fingerprint kit, and a zip drive, just in case the sleigh had a computer. For the next two hours, she chugged can after can of Red Bull, keeping herself awake until she heard a scuffling sound on the roof. Then she grabbed her phone and crept into the hallway.

Her phone had a video recorder on it. Cameras often caught things the human eye couldn't see, and she planned to analyze her footage frame by frame for anything that could prove her theories.

After the hypothesis was formed, the next step of the Scientific Method was to collect data. That could only be done on Christmas Eve in the middle of the night. Climbing out of her window was easy. It was Santa's sleigh, with its lack of padding that was hard.

After she gave up on getting comfortable in the sleigh, she pulled a pair of scissors from her pouch and snipped a long strip from one of Santa's bags. The thin fabric felt like water in her fingers, slippery and silky, nothing like they sold in the sewing section at Walmart. She dropped it into a plastic baggie and mentally prepared a list of how she would analyze it later. She would study the fabric composition, and then she would cut it into pieces and check for water and fire proofing. A thorough scientist was a winning scientist.

She heard a tiny voice echo up the chimney right before a plume of dust escaped out the top. She ducked under the bags before anyone could spot her. A toy box poked out of one of them, its corner stabbing her in the spine. Cellophane crinkled as she tried to shift it to the non-poking side.

"Did you hear that?" asked a tiny, shrill voice.

Tracy froze, holding her breath while listening for the answer.

It came about a minute later when another voice said, "Squirrel. Over in that tree."

"Good eyes," said the first voice. "You ready?"

"Always."

Then, Tracy heard the jingle of bells. She sunk further under the bags, hoping to stay hidden for at least an hour or two. By then it wouldn't matter if she was caught. She'd seen enough movies to know that Santa didn't mind a stowaway every now and then. He'd pat her on the head and take her home, probably with a snow globe or sleigh bell to remember him by. Little would he know that in addition to her trinket, she would have plenty of hard evidence for her project. Pictures. Video footage. Hair samples. Full chemical analysis of his red toy bags.

She smiled to herself and settled in as she heard Santa's boots clomping across the roof. He was here. And it was time to go.

CHAPTER THREE

Tracy

Tracy hadn't anticipated Santa's enormous size. The sleigh lurched as he climbed in, shifting the bags above her, and pushing her shoulder into the wooden floorboards. She clutched her neck pouch to her chest. Every time she'd run through this night in her mind, she'd envisioned only one thing going wrong—Santa accidentally grabbing her neck pouch and gifting it to some well-deserving child. Keeping her limps intact had never been part of the scenario. The back of Santa's seat squished her arm against her body until it went numb. The point of her scissors jutted out the top of her bag and pressed into her thigh. Did scientific experiments have to be so painful?

The next house was only a block away, and while Santa was gone, Tracy had time to shake out her tingling fingers, but little else.

For the next three stops, she kept sneaking her phone up above the bags to take blind shots of what she hoped were the reindeer, but she was so crunched up in the bottom of the sleigh, she couldn't see if she'd gotten anything worth using.

The reindeer weren't helping. They didn't make a single sound, not a snort or a huff to tell her which direction to point the camera. Their silence was good evidence for her theory that they were holograms, but there was also the fact that she couldn't hear anything else. The elves didn't say any more, and Santa never uttered a single "Ho Ho Ho." Who knew a ride with Santa would be so...quiet? An eerie tingle crept up her spine. Or maybe that was the stupid toy box digging into a nerve and making her back go numb.

Her luck finally kicked in at the fourth stop when Santa removed the offending bag and took it down the chimney with him. She twisted her arm behind her back to examine the spot where her skin was screaming. She winced when she touched the tender area. This was for Pim, she reminded herself. What was one little scar compared to getting her cousin back?

With one less bag in the sleigh, Tracy was able to poke her head out and get her first glimpse of the reindeer. They looked pretty much like they did in the movies: antlers, brown and white fur, cow-like faces. But they didn't prance or paw their hooves, or move at all. Even if they were holograms, her grandmother had claimed they were majestic. These guys looked as if they'd been stuffed and mounted, a fancy rooftop decoration instead of the living, breathing creatures they were supposed to be. Was Santa even trying to make them look real?

She snapped about a dozen pictures, but just as she was about to climb out to get some close ups, a yellow plume of smoke appeared out of the chimney signaling Santa's return. Tracy ducked back down into the sleigh. The bag was dropped on top of her once more, minus the toy box with the sharp corners.

As they zoomed off to the next stop, Tracy went down her mental check list of items that she needed. At the next stop, she planned to see if she could get a video of her hand waving through the reindeer projections. Once more of the toys were gone and she had room to maneuver in the sleigh, she could snap some better pictures of them in flight. Would they actually look like they were flying, or would they stay stiff and still like they had been on the rooftop?

Pictures of Santa at his job might be a little harder to get, but not impossible. The hardest things would be the snippet of Santa's beard and saliva sample. Those were vital for the DNA testing. They would prove whether he was human, or some unknown species. For Tracy's hypothesis, she asserted he was something else. Santa was way too old to be human. Besides, how awesome would it be to prove the existence of a new species? With the money from that, she would be able to save Pim and buy her parents a huge mansion, probably in Beverly Hills.

When the sleigh was still once more, and Santa's clomping boots were out of hearing range, Tracy finally heard another voice.

"Show time!" chirped the squeaky elf from before. The sound was followed by a bunch of chitter chatter which she couldn't understand. The voices soon disappeared as the elves presumably slipped down the chimney.

Tracy counted to ten before popping out of the sleigh. She ditched her plan of examining the reindeer at this stop. She couldn't pass up the opportunity to video tape the elves at work. Oddly, the reindeer were gone again.

She figured it had something to do with the projector and searched for a way down to the ground.

The house was two stories, making it too dangerous to drop onto the driveway. And how would she get back up? No trellis to climb, and even if there was one, she doubted it would hold her weight. Only palm trees in the front yard. But in the back yard...Yes! There was an oak tree with several low branches.

She grabbed hold of the first one and swung down

to the ground. There was a large set of windows lining the back of the house. The curtains were open, providing the perfect view of Santa stuffing stockings. Tracy squealed with joy, then clamped a hand over her mouth. She could ruin everything if Santa heard her now. Not to mention the fact that she was trespassing in a stranger's yard. She really needed to be more careful.

Tracy crept up to the window, kneeling in the sand below it in order to blend into the shadows. The Christmas tree inside was brightly lit, providing more than enough light to get her pictures. She snapped a few of Santa, but then realized the real action was happening on the couch. She switched her phone to video and smiled. It was like a live action replay of what happened to her the year she turned eight.

She had slept on the couch with one end of a fishing line wrapped around Santa's milk glass and the other end tied to her pinkie finger. As soon as her finger jerked and she opened her eyes, a shimmery dust blew across her face, producing a vision of cartoon sugar plums dancing in front of her. Now she could watch it happening to another child.

Eight tiny elves moved into her camera's view screen. They looked like cute, wooden puppets, but the way they moved made her shiver. At first she thought it was simply an effect of the camera. They seemed to glide more than walk. But when several of their bodies fuzzed and changed shape briefly to fit between a chair and a wall, she rubbed her eyes, wondering if the Red Bull was wearing off. She shook her head. That was one thing she hadn't anticipated, getting tired so early. Maybe she could find some candy in the sleigh to get another sugar rush.

She blinked a few more times, as she watched the creatures arrange themselves around the couch. A small boy, maybe five or six years old, stretched into a yawn and opened his eyes. Before he saw anything, one of the elves reached into his pocket, pulled out a tiny fist full of something, and blew a cloud of sparkly yellow dust into the boy's face. The boy blinked and rubbed his eyes. Tracy knew exactly what he was seeing—dancing cartoon sugarplums!

This was science fair gold. She wondered if she could spot the street name from the roof so she could find the boy in a day or two and interview him about his experience. Plus, if she brought her mom's Dustbuster, she could vacuum up some of the powder and view it under her microscope.

Tracy squealed again, too excited to cover her mouth this time. She realized her mistake and held her breath for one second. Two seconds. Three. When Santa didn't look her way, she relaxed and vowed to be more careful from now on. Scientists observed with their eyes, not their voices.

CHAPTER FOUR

Santa Command—Control Room 8
December 24th
2342 hours

Phil yelled at the screen. "Who is that? What's she doing?"

A girl down below tapped a couple of keys. All of the stats from Santa's current location appeared on the screen. "Well, she's not Bradley Adams, and he doesn't have a sister." She tapped a few more keys. "Or a cousin. Or any girl neighbors."

"Hang on." Phil scrolled through the archived footage of the night and came up with a still image of a child from a house Santa had visited earlier. He enlarged the image on the view screen and keyed in a command. The child's name appeared across the bottom in white block letters.

Tracy Tam

Walt burst in through the door. His beeper squealed like an Inkling caught in a rat trap. "You took care of this. You said you were positive."

"I...I was!" Phil ordered up the camera outside her bedroom window. It showed a curled up lump lying in her bed, and long black hair trailing out from under the comforter and across her pillow. "See?"

Walt snatched the mouse out of Phil's hand and zoomed in on the picture. His eyes grew wider, accenting the purple vein that was throbbing on his right temple. "I see a bed stuffed with pillows and a wig. Come on, Phil. You were trained to know the difference!"

That's when Phil saw the corner of a pillow sticking out from under the comforter and a kitten curled up where Tracy's head should have been. The wig was a nice touch, he thought. Better than most.

Phil groaned as he dragged his hands down his cheeks. He *had* been trained in this. He'd been top of his class, spotting every trick his teachers had thrown at him. Pillows, dolls, and even one cleverly built life size mannequin. He'd identified them all when no one else could come close. That's why Phil had been given a command job after he'd proven himself in other areas. He was one of the best.

"How much has she seen?" Walt asked.

Phil pressed his hand against his forehead. His

head throbbed. "Too much."

"We're gonna have to wipe her." Walt said this matter of factly, as if the suggestion didn't have far-reaching consequences.

"No. No, we can't." The last time Phil had ordered a wipe on a child, the results had been devastating. He could still remember holding the child's unconscious body in his arms. Walt knew about it, but he kept it quiet. It was something Walt's boss could never know about. "A wipe is too unpredictable."

"Then give me another option."

Phil racked his brain, determined to think of something else. *Anything* else. Vision dust only lasted for a minute or two, and that didn't clear memories; it only obscured the now. Tracy *had* to forget. The Santa legend was sacred.

Walt was right. Even though Tracy hadn't done anything wrong, a mind wipe was the only option. Phil cursed under his breath. Curiosity shouldn't have to be punished.

"Phil, are you going to give the order or should I?"

Tracy, unaware of the camera, was climbing up the tree on her way back to the roof.

Giving Sasha the instructions would be simple. Phil wouldn't have to watch. He could close his eyes until it was done. The Inklings would transport Tracy back to her bedroom, and he could assume everything was fine.

"Phil?"

"I'll handle it," Phil said wearily. This was his screw up. No one else should have this on his conscience. He spoke the order into his head set.

Sasha communicated the instructions to the rest of her crew, and they made their way up the chimney.

CHAPTER FIVE

Tracy

Just as Tracy swung from the tree limb to the roof, a plume of yellow smoke puffed up the chimney. Knowing she only had a few seconds, she scrambled to reach the sleigh, paying no attention to the smoke slithering down to the roof and the eight tiny creatures materializing from it.

She didn't see them grab hold of her shoelaces and yank, sending her sprawling onto her back. She looked up, and there, two inches from her nose, was one of Santa's elves with a sprout-like ponytail on the top of her head.

"This isn't gonna hurt," the elf said as she reached into one of several pouches dangling from her belt. She pulled out a fist full of something which she then held over Tracy's face. A shimmery yellow sparkle dropped from it. Elf dust.

Tracy knew the sugar plum vision would come next, a distraction just long enough for Santa and his crew to get away. But she had come too far to give up this early, and she was ready for it. She jumped to her feet and ran for the sleigh. When Santa reappeared, she would explain her situation. He would see how important this was to her and invite her to join them.

She was only two feet from the sleigh when a six foot tall, green muscular creature jumped in front of her. Based on her multiple readings of Harry Potter, she assumed it was a troll, although she had no idea where he'd come from.

His body was draped in an assortment of leather scraps and covered with warts of various sizes. His head was a small bump on his massive shoulders. His expression looked exactly like that kid in the back of her math class who shrugged and picked his nose every time the teacher asked him a question.

He took a step forward, but she held her ground. She wasn't afraid of the neighbor's pit bull, and she wasn't afraid of this thing. He was a temporary glitch in her plan, one she could probably distract with the sparkles on her cell phone case until Santa arrived. But when she looked in his eyes, she realized he wasn't the dumb creature she had read about in books. His narrow, blue glare made her skin crawl. This guy was smart, and with a slow wink, he let her know it.

Her hands trembled as she repeated in her mind that she wasn't scared. She scurried to the other side of the sleigh, putting it between the two of them. Surely, he wasn't strong enough to crush Santa's sleigh, was he?

The massive creature cocked one side of his mouth into a knowing grin. Three rotten teeth showed between his lips, and the smell of sewer water and Limburger cheese wafted in Tracy's direction. It burned her nose, which she pinched shut.

"I'm not afraid of you." Though she took a step backward as she said it.

She glanced at the chimney. What was taking Santa so long? Wasn't he supposed to protect kids? No wait, that was Batman. But in a world with Santa, elves, and trolls, she took a chance and willed the bat signal to appear in the sky.

While she was looking up, the troll lunged over the sleigh.

Tracy ducked and jumped backwards, tripping over several more elves and landing hard on her back. The fall jarred something loose in her brain, and she couldn't tell if the stars overhead were real or the result of a head injury. She did know her head *hurt*. Her vision blurred for a second before snapping back into focus. Then she guessed what she should have known the moment that speck of dust fell in her eye.

The troll wasn't real. He was a hallucination just like the sugar plums. She felt stupid for not realizing this before.

One of the elves jumped onto her stomach. She tried to brush him off so she could sit up, but his body multiplied in size until he was slightly bigger than her. At that size, he looked less like a cute puppet and more like a haunted tree come to life. She blinked, not trusting anything she saw. It wasn't real. *Magic needs a helping hand.*

The giant elf grabbed her shoulders, pinning her to the roof. The troll lumbered around the sleigh and knelt down beside Tracy. His rock-like fist hovered over her face while another sparkle drifted toward her eye.

"Stop it!"

Tracy turned her head to avoid the dust. Her brain throbbed with the motion, and she didn't know if she could trust her eyes anymore. She trusted her instincts though, and they said to get away.

Before any more dust escaped the troll's fist, Tracy grabbed the elf's arms, twisted them and shifted her weight, propelling him off of her and into the troll. Both went tumbling across the roof in a tangle of rapidly shrinking arms and legs. She rolled in the opposite direction, barely stopping herself from plunging over the roof's edge.

She pushed herself to her feet and watched in

awe as both the large elf and the troll assumed the shape of Santa's elves. And there were more of them, eight total. She rubbed her fists in her eyes trying the remove the dust. When she looked again, the semi circle of creatures was still there, advancing toward her as they shifted into a pack of wolves. Several of them snarled, revealing razor sharp teeth. Finally, she admitted to herself that she was afraid.

She peeked over her shoulder at the concrete driveway. It seemed so far away. Even worse, she had no idea where she was. She could be in Orlando, or Tampa, or Miami, with nowhere to run and no way to get home. Still, that was a better option than the growling pack of wolves that was one leap away from tearing her to shreds. Hallucination or not, all she could think about was getting home and away from these nightmare creatures.

She took a deep breath and jumped.

CHAPTER SIX

Santa Command—Control Room 8
December 24th
2352 hours

Phil watched with horror as Tracy plummeted to the concrete driveway. She landed with a crack, her arm twisted unnaturally beneath her. The wolves jumped off the roof, transforming back into Inklings in mid-air and sprouting wings in the process. They landed softly beside Tracy, each one of them looking to Sasha, who pulled a handful of dust from her pocket and stepped up to Tracy's body.

Tracy's still image filled the entire twenty foot screen. In addition to the broken arm, she had a line of blood running from her forehead, down her cheek, and into her hair.

Phil looked to his boss, who had turned away from the screen, occupying himself in some task that didn't really need to be done. He knew what Walt was thinking. This was Paige Murphy all over again.

Phil had been the one to see Paige's body go slack. Horrified at what he'd done, Phil had transported himself to her house and woken Paige's family in the middle of the night. He didn't tell them the truth though. He claimed to be driving home from a party when he saw her lying motionless on her driveway. Paige's bedroom window had been open, and her parents assumed she had fallen while trying to spot Santa. Paige, of course, wasn't talking, and it was likely she never would again.

The memory of Paige was enough to give Phil a lifetime of nightmares. No secret was worth adding another child to his list.

Sasha's fist hovered over Tracy's face, her fingers opening one by one. A speck of dust drifted onto the girl's eyes. And then another speck.

"Stop!" Phil ordered into the Inkling's ear bud, knowing full well the trouble he was about to dump on himself. "I rescind my order. Transport her back here."

CHAPTER SEVEN

Tracy

Sound came to Tracy first—muffled tinkling that made her think someone was talking to her, but she couldn't hear the person through all of the static buzzing in her head. As she rubbed the sleep from her eyes, she realized the static wasn't in her head. It was coming from the black speaker that hung in one of the corners. "Frosty the Snowman" was playing, and the lyrics danced through Tracy's mind.

The second thing that came to Tracy was her injuries. She remembered jumping from the roof as those things chased her and the terrible pain that had shot through her arm. Now, her arm was encased in a yellow sleeve that wasn't anything like the cast she'd gotten in 3rd grade after jumping off of her swing set, playing Superman. This cast felt like it was made out of jelly. When she touched it, a tingly feeling shot through her bone, chasing away the pain. There was no bandage on her forehead. It didn't hurt either, although there was a small amount of dried blood clumped in her hair.

But how had she ended up in what appeared to be Santa's dressing room?

She tapped her pointer finger against her chin as her scientific mind whirled into high gear. They had wanted the boy to fall back asleep, so she assumed they'd made him see sugar plums. What if they had wanted to make her afraid, scare her away so she'd go back home? That's why they had showed her trolls and wolves. She shivered at the memory. They hadn't expected her to get hurt, and when she did, Santa gave them no choice but to bring her to his house and bandage her up. That had to be it!

Once Tracy had all of that figured out, she felt a lot better, especially since being at his house meant she'd be able to gather even more evidence for her experiment. With that in mind, she sat up on the overstuffed red couch and pressed her palms against her eyelids once more to make sure she wasn't dreaming. No, this was more than a dream. It was a dream come true! She was in Santa's dressing room complete with a Christmas tree shaped armoire and a gold framed mirror mounted on the wall opposite her.

Around the mirror hung at least a dozen

motivational posters. Some of them were the same ones her English teacher had displayed in her classroom with captions like, "Teamwork: Many hands, many minds, one goal." Others looked like they had been custom made for Santa, like the one with him placing a pink bicycle under a tree that said, "Christmas: You're doing it right." Tracy laughed as she pictured Santa chanting, "Go, Team, Go!" as he put on his hat every Christmas Eve.

The room had one window and if she had any doubt about where she was, it was erased as she looked through the glass into the surrounding forest. Nestled between two pine trees, there was a candy cane striped pole with a sign that read:

North Pole
Population: 2 humans, 582 elves, 8 reindeer

Snowflakes the size of cotton balls floated past the window, blanketing the ground in a perfect layer of ice. Tracy was enchanted. She had never seen snow and desperately wanted to see what it felt like. She tried to lift the window. At first, it didn't budge because she could only use one hand, but then she put her shoulder into it and raised it high enough to stick her fingers under it. When she did, the scene on the window fizzled into static like a broken TV. Tracy jumped backwards, letting the window slam shut. The snow returned, same as it was before.

"What the—"

She ran her fingers along the ledge, and in the right hand corner she found a thin wire painted white to match the rest of the ledge. That wire connected to one on the window. She lifted the pane again, breaking the connection between the two wires. The scene fizzled just like before. This time, she kept lifting the window. It was heavy, but she got it high enough where she could turn her head sideways and get her left eye close enough to the crack to see outside. And she saw...

Nothing. No snow. No lights. There was a forest, but it looked nothing like the enchanted landscape she had seen through the window. No evergreens, just tall, bare trees that felt like they were crowding the building, reaching for it with giant claws. An icy wind rushed through the crack, and Tracy dropped the window again.

More illusions? What was going on? This was no longer holograms for the benefit of people peeking out their windows. This went deeper than any of that.

She grew a little frightened, but not enough to cry or panic. She just kept reminding herself that being at Santa's house was like being the first man on the moon. She had to think like a scientist. It had been a warm winter. Maybe they hadn't had any snow and the scene on the window was just to help Santa get in a Christmas-y mood.

She went to examine the rest of the room. There was a table beside the couch with an origami-looking reindeer lamp. The dim light shined down on a few photos of Santa and his wife. One shot was taken at the beach with Santa wearing an old fashioned red bathing suit and holding a surf board. It was just like the post cards they sold in all of the tourist shops back home. That bit of familiarity settled Tracy's thoughts.

She moved on to the armoire. Before she touched the brass door knob, she pulled four items from her neck pouch: cocoa powder, a white index card, a paintbrush, and tape. She used the items to lift a smudgy fingerprint from the knob. She didn't know what information Santa's fingerprint would give her, but it didn't hurt to have it.

Once her evidence was stored safely in the pouch, she twisted the brass door knob and pulled it open. Inside, hung three identical Santa suits. That all seemed pretty normal, but what stood out was the tag inside the collar. Tracy had expected it to read something like, "Sewn with love by Mrs. Claus." Instead it had a name stitched in sparkly green thread: E. Higgens. It reminded her of how her mother had sewn a label that said "T. Tam" into all of her clothes last year for summer camp.

Who was E. Higgens? Was he the one who made the coat? Elf Higgens?

Tracy reached into her pocket for her phone. She needed a picture of this. When the phone wasn't in her pocket, she began to panic.

She ran back to the couch. "No! No! No!" she said while tossing the candy cane shaped throw pillows onto the carpet and digging between the couch cushions. "No! Where is it? Where is it?" She sunk down onto the sofa, her bottom lip trembling as she knew where it had to be—shattered in a million pieces on the little boy's driveway all the way back in Florida.

"No," she whispered into the chocolate scented air.

She flopped back on the couch, wondering if she had any hope of completing the project without her phone. Those pictures were at the heart of her project. Her eyes drifted once more to Santa's photos on the table.

Maybe she could take those photos with her. Or maybe...Tracy touched her finger to Mrs. Claus' chubby smile, and an idea settled in her mind. Santa obviously wasn't home, but maybe his wife was.

CHAPTER EIGHT

Santa Command—Control Room 8
December 25th
0022 hours

Phil focused on number crunching, trying to gain lost seconds here and there. If Santa skipped one toy every three houses, he had a good chance of making up that time by 0530, which was when the Santa program ended.

Phil was so busy, in fact, that he had put Tracy out of his mind. She was sleeping the night away in a dressing room, the only part of Santa Command she would ever see. The Inklings had worked their magic on her injuries, and when the time came to take her home, she would be good as new. Until then, Beth, who maintained the children's wish lists, was watching the video feed of the girl from her office. Once Tracy woke up, Beth would talk to her and convince her she'd been to Santa's house. Then, Beth would make Tracy promise never to tell another living soul. He figured this would be done through a pinky swear. That's what little girls did, didn't they?

He had done the right thing. He didn't need to worry. Walt didn't need to worry. Phil's plan was solid. He was an expert in predicting how kids would react in different situations. Tracy would be no exception.

CHAPTER NINE

Tracy

The door was locked. She tried it about a hundred times, hoping for a different result, but it stayed locked no matter what she did. She even tried picking it with a paperclip, but that only worked in the movies. What good was packing an emergency supply kit if it didn't help in emergencies?

She folded her arms across her chest and huffed as she sagged back against the door. If she was going to find Mrs. Claus and grill her for information, she had only one option. She marched over to the armoire, where she pulled out one of E. Higgens' handmade coats. But before she put it on, she grabbed hold of the name tag in the collar, ripped it out, then slipped it into her neck pouch. Evidence, because she doubted anyone would let her take the coat home with her.

The coat hung down to her knees, but when she

tightened up the black leather belt, it fit more like a dress. More importantly, it would keep her from freezing to death in the Arctic as she searched for another room from the outside.

She grabbed the lip of the window and heaved upward, putting way more muscle into it than she had before. It moved a few inches, but she forgot to be careful, and her broken arm screamed in pain.

"Ow! Ow! Ow! OW!" She jumped up and down, clutching her arm to her chest.

Then, she remembered to be quiet. Santa didn't want her leaving the room, so he'd probably frown on her going out the window. But gathering evidence was essential to saving Pim. Surely, Santa would forgive her, especially if she got everything she needed before he found out she was gone.

Tracy pushed the window up, taking a lot more care with her arm this time, and climbed through it. As she popped out onto the crunchy dried up grass, the window slammed shut behind her. She whirled around and nearly fell over. Santa's house was gone! It was as if she were standing in a small clearing with the skeletons of dead trees closing in on her.

This was the second time that night she had been truly afraid. What happened to the house? How was she going to find her way back in? How was she going to find her way home?

She closed her eyes and forced herself to calm down. There had to be a rational explanation. Buildings didn't just disappear. It was probably some trick of light or mirrors designed to keep anyone from accidentally stumbling onto Santa's house. She hadn't heard of many people hiking around the North Pole looking for Santa, but if she had been brought there, then others had probably been brought there too. Santa had to have some sort of plan to ensure people couldn't find their way back.

With trembling hands, she reached out in front of her, swishing them through the air until her fingertips brushed against the cool concrete. She pressed her palms and her forehead against the wall and sighed with relief.

The house was still there. It was simply...hidden.

It felt strange, because it looked like she was leaning against absolutely nothing, but the wall was there. The scratchy concrete told her so.

Once she knew the building hadn't gone anywhere, she ran her hands along the wall, trying to find the window again. She had no intention of going back in that way, but she needed to know that it was an option.

She found the window. The problem was, there was no way to open it again. No edge that she could tuck her fingers under, and no way to muscle it open by pushing up on the glass. She hoped the other windows weren't like that, but figured they probably were. Well, maybe she could find a back door or something.

Tracy held her breath as she scuffled forward, dragging her fingers along the wall, searching for an opening. The North Pole was supposed to be wondrous, but this place reminded her more of a graveyard at midnight than a magical toy shop.

The silence made her ears feel like they'd been stuffed with cotton. Nothing skittered. Nothing squeaked. Every now and then, a slight wind blew, and the bare tree branches scratched against each other, rattling Tracy's nerves. Even the building felt rough and uninviting. She scrunched up inside the red velvet coat, but it wasn't enough to stop the chill from spreading through her bones.

As the minutes piled on top of her, she continued inching her way down the building.

Maybe my window was the only way in, she thought. The night was beginning to feel like an episode of Doctor Who. Elves that turned into trolls. Windows that weren't really windows. Buildings that disappeared when you looked at them. What if she really wasn't at Santa's workshop? What if she'd fallen into some other dimension or had been kidnapped by some alien masquerading as Santa?

She was just about to let her imagination take her to a different planet when a large column of light appeared in the middle of the forest. It was maybe a football field away, and it shot up into the sky as if the ground had opened up. To confirm her theory, Santa's sleigh whooshed overhead, zooming straight toward the light.

Well, that's more like it.

Tracy ran through the trees, ducking as the branches snagged on her coat and pulled at her hair. Santa's sleigh hovered in the beam of light for half a second, then lowered down, disappearing behind a large outcropping of rock. By the time she reached the spot where the light had appeared, both it and the sleigh were gone. In their place sat a small, perfectly still pond. A cave framed one side of it, and dangling above the entrance, reaching down toward the water, was a line of icicles that looked like a frozen chandelier. The icicles were too perfect. Each one was roughly the same size, and they were spaced evenly apart.

Something about the pond was off too. She had never seen one that calm, and it didn't smell like earth or mold. It smelled like that car factory her parents had once taken her to—oil and metal. She approached the edge and swished her hand through the water, finding exactly what she expected. The water wasn't there. Another trick of light, just like Santa's house.

She reached down further and instead of finding mud, her hand touched something hard and smooth. She tapped it with her fingernails, and it echoed slightly, like a tin drum. Tracy smiled, the kind of smile where crazy ideas start to make sense. She held no hope of getting the ground to open up for her, but she didn't think she needed to.

Those icicles stretched down just like a gate, but they didn't quite reach the surface of the water. Lifting up the hem of her coat, just in case, Tracy waded into the pretend pond. The illusion swirled around her ankles, but her assumption held true. There wasn't a single drop of water in that clearing.

When she got to the icicles, she looked closely at them, noticing each one had a thin, metal tube running the length of it. Yep, those icicles had a purpose. They certainly were real though. And cold.

She sat down in the "water" and sucked in a deep breath, holding it in puffed out cheeks. She knew she didn't need to, but the illusion was just so real. Then, she laid down and rolled under the wall of icicles.

On the other side, she sat up, still holding her breath. No alarms. No flashing lights to warn Santa of intruders. They had taken a great deal of care to create a fake world, but it didn't seem to go beyond that. Well, that was good at least. Tracy let out her breath and stood up.

From inside the cave, it was easy to find the stairs carved out of the wall at the back. She took one last look around to make sure there weren't any cameras or trip wires, then started down the stairs.

CHAPTER TEN

Tracy

Tracy stood at the top of a metal staircase high above the warehouse floor. A huge circular platform descended with a loud squeal into the center of the room. On it sat Santa in his now-empty sleigh, and his eight reindeer. Surrounding the platform were hundreds of gray metal shelves, each ten or fifteen feet high, stuffed with wrapped packages. The shelves stood in long, neat rows. Each row was labeled with a three digit number, reminding Tracy of the huge library downtown. Many of them were only half-full, or altogether empty. She assumed the presents were all for this year. That had been one of her points for the project. How did Santa fit all of those toys in his sleigh? Now she knew. He didn't. He reloaded.

On instinct, Tracy reached for her cell phone before remembering it wasn't there. She cursed herself for jumping off that stupid roof. She *needed* her phone, and she needed it *now*.

Or did she?

She didn't need her phone specifically, just a camera. And in a warehouse full of Christmas presents, there was bound to be dozens of them.

Tracy raced down the stairs and ducked into the first row she came to. She felt a moment of guilt for what she was about to do, but when she thought about Pim and the reason she was doing this, her actions seemed justified. Still, she didn't want to randomly start ripping apart boxes. She had to do this methodically. She quickly gathered a small pile of presents that were about the size and weight of a camera, then she started opening, peeling back just a little bit of paper so that it looked like it had been accidentally ripped. In the fourth box, she found exactly what she was looking for, a digital camera that came with batteries, so it didn't need to be charged. She clutched it to her chest and smiled, silently praising herself for her idea.

By the time Tracy had set up her new camera, the platform had disappeared behind the towering shelves, so she darted from aisle to aisle until she found a hiding place with a good view. She rounded a corner just in time to see a line of about twenty of those elf things marching single file to the sleigh, all wearing tiny yellow hard hats. The creatures each held a bundle of presents so large, they looked like ants carrying elephants.

She snapped a dozen pictures as one by one, the elves stepped onto a small black square on the platform beside the sleigh. Off to the side, another elf pressed a red button set into a control panel, and the square lifted to the top of the sleigh. There, the first elf arranged presents in one of Santa's red bags, then was lowered back to the platform.

The elves continued on, with their assembly line until Santa's sleigh was once again loaded. Through it all, Santa and his reindeer remained perfectly still, each of them wearing that same glazed over look that she'd seen on those figures in the wax museum she'd been to out in California. Her skin prickled as she imagined touching Santa's face and feeling nothing but lifeless wax.

No! she reprimanded herself. There had to be a reasonable explanation for this. This was the longest night of the year for Santa. Maybe he was simply taking a quick nap. Her friend, Macy, had once brought a picture to school of her little brother sleeping with his eyes open. He looked pretty much like Santa did now, except she couldn't tell if Santa was drooling like Macy's brother did.

A few seconds later, the elf at the control panel punched another button. The ceiling opened again with a squeal of metal scraping metal, and the platform rose back into the night sky. As it rose, some stray pieces of the elves' yellow dust drifted off the sleigh and floated to the ground.

Once the ceiling shut, the elves all scuttled off in different directions.

Tracy slid the camera into her shirt pocket and made her way through the stacks. She could have climbed back up the way she'd come, but she was betting on there being a door somewhere that led back into Santa's house. She still believed Mrs. Claus was the person she needed.

As Tracy picked her way through the maze of shelves, she spotted a yellow dust spec sitting on one of the presents. It almost blended in with the gold foil wrapping paper, but the sparkle caught her eye. Always a scientist, she realized the opportunity when she saw it. Very carefully, she pinched the dust spec between her fingers. It felt warm, and it tingled between her fingertips. She couldn't wait to get back home and analyze it.

She pulled her neck pouch out from under her shirt and searched it for a plastic baggie. She had already contaminated her evidence by touching it. The sooner she had it in its own container, the better. She zipped the dust spec into the plastic bag, but she quickly realized her mistake. Once the dust touched the plastic, it started to glow. Then, it pulsed and expanded. She knew that certain chemicals reacted badly with others. Maybe something in the dust didn't agree with the plastic.

She wanted to open it and get that dust out, but the bag grew hot in her hands. Volcano hot. All she could think about, while the bag heated up and the dust expanded, was getting it out of her hands and getting away.

She quickly stuffed it into a crack between two presents and ran. Before she got halfway down the aisle, the bag exploded. There was no smoke or fire, but there was a loud bang and a gaping hole where about a dozen presents should have been.

She might have been worried that someone had heard the explosion, but at that exact moment, the ceiling split open again with a deafening squeal.

Tracy forgot about the dust and looked up. Santa couldn't be back already. Could he?

As she looked toward the ceiling, she knew she was wrong. Santa and his team were descending once again with an empty sleigh. She figured it had only been about a minute and a half since he left. That made no sense at all. In the half an hour she'd ridden with him, he hadn't managed to empty the sleigh.

Her mind was busy trying to come up with a logical explanation when she noticed Santa's beard. Less than a minute before, it had been as curly as a ribbon. Now, it was as straight as her own hair. Her mouth gaped open at the sight. She had just discovered another one of magic's "helping hands."

"Impressive, isn't it?" said a voice behind her.

CHAPTER ELEVEN

Santa Command—Loading Dock
December 25th
0054 hours

Phil stepped forward. Beth stood beside him. It was her fault Tracy had escaped the dressing room, so she insisted on coming along to help.

Tracy's eyes darted between Phil and Beth. It wasn't the kind of look children give when they're trying to come up with an excuse. Phil got the sense he was being studied, kind of like the personality test he'd endured when first coming to work for Santa Command. It unnerved him to be analyzed like that by a ten-year-old girl.

When Tracy was satisfied, she squared her shoulders and lifted her chin. "I believe I have an appointment with Mrs. Claus."

Phil had intended to utter some adult-sounding

phrase like, "You shouldn't be in here," grab her by the shoulders, and march her back to a safe zone where she wouldn't see anything "unusual." But the self-assured tone in Tracy's voice made Phil's words fizzle out before they reached his lips. He clutched his hands in front of him, wishing for the comfort of a computer keyboard. His life's work involved squaring off with children, but he always did it from a behind a control panel. Going one-on-one was an entirely different skill. Fortunately, Beth was raising her eleven-year-old nephew and had no trouble handling the situation.

"Absolutely, but first," she put her hands on Tracy's shoulders and turned her toward the door, "we need to get you out of here. None of us should be in here. It's a hard hat zone after all." She tapped a yellow and black striped sign on one of the shelves confirming exactly what she said.

Phil followed behind them as Beth led Tracy into the hallway, half impressed by Beth's ability to do what he hadn't, and half shocked that Beth had promised Tracy she would meet Mrs. Claus. How did she plan on making *that* happen?

As they walked, Beth introduced both herself and Phil.

He mumbled a "Hello," but otherwise didn't interrupt.

"How's your arm doing?" Beth asked.

"Um…" Tracy slid up the arm of her Santa coat. Her cast was a reminder that Phil was part of the reason she'd been injured. He was glad they were able to fix that at least. "Good, I guess."

"Does it still hurt?"

Tracy poked the cast in several places. "No, not anymore."

"Then, let's take that off."

They all stopped in the hallway while Beth slid her finger inside the cast and pushed a button located near Tracy's wrist. The cast dissolved, leaving nothing but a freshly healed arm.

"Wow!" Tracy wiggled her fingers. "How'd you do that? Was it some sort of heat soluble fabric?"

"I'm not sure what you're talking about." Beth turned around and continued walking.

Tracy scrambled to catch up, her curiosity piqued. "That button you pushed. It must have sent heat through the cast and made it disappear."

Beth considered that, carefully thinking out her answer.

Good, Phil thought. *You have to be on your toes when it comes to this kid.*

Beth finally said, "Did you feel any heat?"

Tracy touched her arm as if she were trying to remember. "No."

"Okay," Beth said as if the matter was settled.

"How about we say it was magic?"

"How about we don't?" Tracy whipped out a tiny notebook and pen and scribbled something down. "I've given you my hypothesis—"

"And I've proven your hypothesis incorrect. When that happens, you need to modify it."

Tracy paused mid step and let that sink in. Her pen hovered over her paper. "Modify it to what?"

"I gave you an alternative theory." Beth took Tracy's notebook and scribbled the word "magic."

"And I denied it."

"Why?"

"Because magic doesn't exist." Tracy took the notebook back and crossed out Beth's answer.

"Hm, I've heard that before."

Phil marveled at their banter. He was beginning to see what brought Tracy to Santa Command. She was one of those kids who needed to understand everything. He had been one of those kids, which eventually led him to his job.

Tracy frowned. "You still haven't answered my question."

"I have, but you haven't accepted the answer." Beth continued walking.

They passed several of the control rooms, including the one Phil had been working in before Tracy arrived. Several dozen employees rushed past them, seeking out different control rooms and different Santas. Fortunately, Walt wasn't anywhere around. He would ask them to explain themselves. How could Phil do that when he didn't have a clue where Beth was taking them?

Of course, Tracy would be the one to ask. "Where are we going?"

Beth led them down a side hallway. "I'm taking you to see something more concrete. But I guarantee you won't find scientific answers for everything you see tonight."

"I bet I will," Tracy said.

"I don't make bets." Beth stopped in front of a door with a keypad lock above the handle. "Ah, here we are."

Phil, who had been following along like Tracy, stopped short when he saw what room they were standing in front of. He suddenly understood what Beth meant about meeting Mrs. Claus.

He pulled Beth around the corner and lowered his voice to a whisper. "This is a very bad idea."

"Maybe," she said, "but what do you think she's going to do if we lock her in that dressing room again?"

"Sneak out," he admitted.

"Exactly. You brought her here. You need to make sure she has enough information that she knows to keep quiet."

Beth was right. A little information was dangerous. Tracy might blab to all of her friends. But if she knew why she couldn't talk about it, then maybe they could turn this disaster around.

"Fine," he said, "but we're not telling Walt about this."

CHAPTER TWELVE

Tracy

The sign on the door said "Main Frame." Tracy knew enough about computers to know what that meant. This was where it all happened. But even if she didn't know that, the sweat beads on Phil's forehead told her she was about to walk into something big. Would she see how the illusions worked? Would she meet E. Higgens? Would she find out why there were two adults in business clothes working at the North Pole? She hadn't had the chance to work the last one out in her head, and now she didn't have to. Beth had taken her to the exact place she needed to go. All of their secrets were held in this one room. It must be huge!

Tracy placed her hand on the doorknob. "You know, I've got a lot more questions."

"I'm sure you do," Beth said as she punched the code into the keypad. "And we're going to do our best to answer them."

"Thanks." Tracy opened the door, ready to gasp in awe. But when she saw what was inside, her hopes plummeted.

The room was smaller than her parents' closet and just as boring. There was a plain wooden desk pressed up against one wall, with a single large computer sitting in the middle. A cartoon screen saver of a roaring fireplace danced across the monitor. The room didn't even have a window. Where were the flashing lights? Where were the elves frantically pushing buttons in order to keep Christmas from collapsing?

Tracy touched a finger to one of the dull, gray walls. It was solid. The room was no illusion. "This is it?"

Beth pulled one corner of her mouth up in a smile. Tracy recognized that look as one her mother used when she meant, "You're gonna be surprised." The last time her mom had used that look, it ended in a trip to the dentist and three fillings. Tracy hoped Beth did not share her mother's sick sense of humor.

"Have a seat." Beth nudged Tracy into the chair, then knelt beside her and shook the mouse. The computer whirred and grunted for half a minute before finally coming to life. When it did, only a pale blue desktop appeared. It wasn't even as fancy as the ones at school. They at least had an owl, the school's mascot, as the background.

Tracy studied Beth, wondering what the woman was hiding. None of these puzzle pieces fit together. If Tracy didn't make sense of them soon, these people were going to ship her back home. She'd be no closer to helping Pim than she had been two months ago.

"This is *nice*." Tracy emphasized the word "nice" so Beth would know she was being sarcastic. "But when are you going to show me the real stuff?"

Beth tapped the flat screen monitor with her pointer finger. "You don't think this is real?"

"Oh, I think the computer is real, but you guys have jet propelled sleighs, television screens on windows, and an entire underground loading area. You're high tech, and this room is not. Whatever you're going to show me here will be just as fake as Santa Claus."

Beth paused for a moment. Her forehead crinkled like she was thinking very hard what to say next. "Tracy, I'm asking you to trust me. Can you do that?"

Tracy didn't know Beth well enough to answer that, but she did know the room had been locked. It had to hold something important. Tracy turned back to the computer screen. "What's on this thing?"

"Magic," Beth said. When Tracy rolled her eyes, Beth clarified. "Or what other people see as magic. These are the...mostly...logical explanations for what you've seen tonight."

That was more like it. "My science teacher says I

have a mind for logic."

Beth let out a soft laugh. "I totally believe that."

Tracy smiled at the compliment. She was beginning to like Beth. "So," Tracy said as she settled into her seat, "are there only two Santas, or are there more?"

"Later," Beth promised. "First, we'll start with this." She opened up Google Earth and pointed to the image of the planet from space. "Where do you think we are?"

Tracy eyed Beth. "That sounds like a trick question."

Beth placed Tracy's hand on the mouse and said, "Go on."

Tracy shrugged and moved the pointer to where she thought the North Pole would be located. Somewhere in Canada maybe. But after zooming in, all she found were trees and a large chunk of ice. Beth shook her head, so Tracy zoomed in on a couple of other places. After three tries, Tracy finally gave up. "Well, it's around there somewhere. The building is invisible, so it wouldn't show up on a radar, would it?"

"One of those statements is true." Beth took the mouse, zoomed out, and rotated the globe toward the southern United States. When she found the right spot, she zoomed back in, focusing on a forest somewhere in northern...

"Alabama?" Tracy exclaimed. "Why the heck are we in Alabama?" Then Tracy remembered she had no proof that's where they actually were. It wasn't like she could see the building. Tracy pursed her lips. "How do I know you're telling me the truth?"

"Look at the evidence. You know it's not cold enough. You know those aren't the right kind of trees. You know there's been something off from the moment you woke up here. This," she waved toward the screen, "is one of the explanations you're looking for. There are twenty four different Santa Commands in the United States. We are simply one branch."

"Let's pretend I believe you," Tracy said. From what she'd seen, it was possible. "What other explanations are you going to give me?"

Beth looked back to Phil, who'd been hovering in the corner, looking very worried. "Can you pull up Mrs. Claus? I don't have access."

Phil pushed himself away from the wall like he'd been glued to it. "I can." He could have said "I'd rather die first," and it would have sounded the same.

"Are you ready to see the biggest secret of all?" Beth asked.

Whatever doubts Tracy had about the computer, those words made Tracy's heart leap in excitement. She looked Beth in the dead center of her eyes, and knew that despite her comments about magic, that woman was the real deal. "Yes."

"All right then. Phil, show her Mrs. Claus."

CHAPTER THIRTEEN

Tracy

Tracy stood up and let Phil take the seat in front of the computer. He may have looked young, but his shoulders curled like he carried more years than her dad. He hunched over the computer, his head held up by one hand while he worked the mouse with the other. He mumbled things Tracy couldn't quite understand, although they sounded an awful lot like words she wasn't allowed to say. How did anyone get to be such a grump?

Phil double clicked on a folder on the desktop. A login box appeared with the user name already populated—Mary Christmas. Phil glanced at the hallway to make sure no one was coming, then typed in the password. Tracy watched his fingers very carefully as he entered Nicholas343.

Numerous files popped up with titles like The List,

Inkling Profiles, Sleigh Routes, Employee Selection, Holographic Imagery, and Inventions. Phil skipped all of those, going straight to a file labeled Mrs. Claus. He double clicked that, and a list of names appeared.

Tracy gasped when she recognized one of them. "Edward Higgens."

"Do you know him?" Phil asked.

Tracy felt like she was at school, being asked a question she didn't know the answer to. "No, well, it's just...um..." She stuffed her hands in the Santa coat's pockets.

"Ah." Beth got it before Phil did. "The name tag."

Phil nodded, then clicked on Edward's name. A full profile opened up, complete with a picture of a man who looked very much like Santa, one with a curly beard.

Name: Edward Cornelius Higgens

Age: 75

Address: 11 Maple Drive, Sarasota, FL 34230

Occupation: Retired air force pilot

Recruitment date: July 31, 2009

Recruiter: Phil Marlin

Side effects to Santa program: None

"Side effects?" Tracy asked.

"Nausea, vomiting, disorientation, memories of the sleigh ride..." Phil might have kept going with his list if Tracy hadn't stopped him.

"Memories. Are you saying this guy pretends to be Santa, then you take away his memory?"

Phil sighed. "It's more complicated than that. You wouldn't understand."

Tracy placed her hands on her hips and cocked her head in a way that would have gotten her sent straight to her room if she'd done it in front of her mom. "I'm ten. Not an idiot. Try me."

Phil looked to Beth like he was asking for help. The two of them exchanged a few silent gestures which Tracy took to mean they were fighting over who talked next.

"Oh, for Pete's sake. *Someone* answer me."

"Hey," Beth said. "Cut the attitude. We're trying to figure out the best way to address this."

"Which is not at all," Phil insisted. Again, he glanced at the door. "If Walt finds out, it doesn't matter what you think or how much you trust this girl, he is going to wipe her mind."

Beth didn't speak for a long time, and Tracy realized it was because the woman was scared.

Now, Tracy was scared. Who was Walt? "What's a mind wipe?"

"It's nothing you have to worry about," Beth finally answered, but she didn't seem too sure about it. She shooed Phil out of the chair, and he went back to lean against the wall with his arms folded across his chest.

He looked like a statue that was about to crumble. For the first time, Tracy wondered if Santa's place was safe after all. Well, if they were in Alabama, it wasn't really Santa's place, was it? Who owned this operation? Who was in charge here? And if they wiped her mind, how badly would it hurt?

Beth took over the seat and babbled on about the process of choosing Santas. Tracy only half listened. What was the point if they were going to make her forget anyway? She had worked so hard to save Pim, and now instead of saving her, she'd gotten herself kidnapped. Would she ever see Pim again? And would she remember her if she did?

Tracy's knees started to shake. She clutched the edge of the desk, and her stomach clenched itself into a little ball. She felt herself sinking to the ground.

"Um, Beth…" Phil interrupted.

Beth stopped her monologue long enough to look at Tracy. Her eyes grew wide with horror. "Oh, honey. No."

Tracy sat on the floor with her knees folded against her chest and her arms wrapped around them. Her mind felt as vacant as the pretend Santas.

Beth slid down to the floor beside Tracy and scooped her up into her arms. "Sweetie, no. We didn't mean to scare you. It's just, you've thrown us for a loop here. We're still trying to figure things out."

"Are you..." Asking the question meant that she might get an answer she didn't want to hear, but she had to ask it anyway. "Are you going to let me go home, or am I trapped here?"

"Trapped is such an ugly word," said a squeaky voice from the doorway, "but I'd say it's accurate."

CHAPTER FOURTEEN

Tracy

The elf wasn't as cute as the ones back at the house. Then again, the ones at the house hadn't been so cute either once they turned into wolves. What was this guy going to turn into?

Phil jumped to attention. "What are you doing here, Erlek?"

"Walt sent me because you weren't back yet." A sly smile spread across the elf's face. "I think he will be very interested to know what I found out."

Beth slipped a hard mask onto her face. Yet, her arms were still gently wrapped around Tracy. "What? That we found Tracy lost and scared? That we were comforting her?"

"Inside the main computer room?"

"She didn't see anything." Beth spoke calmly, as if she hadn't just showed Tracy the biggest secret in the world. Of course, it helped that Beth had put the computer in sleep mode before she slipped to the floor. Once again, it showed nothing but the crackling fireplace. Because of that, Tracy knew that she could trust Beth. "Tracy woke up in a strange place, wandered off, and got lost. When we found her, she was in hysterics because one of your brothers scared her half to death. This was the closest room we could find to get her away and calm her down. Fat lot of good that did. You've gone and freaked her out again."

Tracy knew a cue when she heard it. She buried her face in Beth's shoulder and wailed. In truth, the cries were only half-fake. She remembered what those elf things did to her on the roof. Through her tears, she kept one eye on the creature in case he decided to turn into a dragon or a rattlesnake.

Erlek folded his wrinkly brown arms across his chest.

"Whatever," he said with a sneer. "Walt said no more stalling. He wants you in his office, and I have a feeling I know why." He patted the tiny pouch of dust hanging from his belt.

Phil dropped his head back against the wall and closed his eyes.

Tracy guessed what was inside the pouch. They might wipe the Santas' minds every Christmas Eve, but nobody was coming near her with that stuff. She needed her memory of this night more than she ever needed anything in the world. She had to trust that she had enough evidence to win the fair, because with the elf stepping toward her, she could only think of one out. Tracy let out another wail. "I want to go hooome."

"Of course you do." Beth smoothed Tracy's long black hair, then addressed Erlek with her eyes narrowed. "A wipe is completely unnecessary, and I won't let it happen. Tracy understands how important it is to keep our secret. Don't you, Tracy?"

Tracy lifted her head and gave a pitiful nod.

"It's true," Phil said. "She does." He didn't sound quite as convinced as Beth, and Tracy wished he'd just kept his mouth shut.

Erlek returned Beth's glare with one of his own, one that made a shiver run down Tracy's spine. "Oh, she may understand, but you don't. Walt wants to see all three of you. You're done at Santa Command."

And with that announcement, even Beth lost her cool.

CHAPTER FIFTEEN

Tracy

"Out in the hall, now!" Beth pushed herself to her feet, leaving Tracy in a lump on the floor.

Tracy got up to follow her, but when Beth gave her a look that said, "Stay here," Tracy sank back to the floor and did her best to look pathetic. That involved putting on the puppy dog eyes that her dad fell for every time.

Erlek humphed and shuffled into the hall. Phil followed, and Beth brought up the rear, shutting the door behind her. But just before she did so, she poked her head back through the doorway to say, "Don't worry. Everything will be fine."

Tracy wasn't worried anymore, because she spotted something on the ceiling that made her smile. With some quick thinking, she had a revised two-part plan.

Beth's voice carried through the closed door. "... only place we're taking her is home."

Then, there was some mumbling. Tracy was dying to know what was being said about her, but the computer was just sitting there, hers for the hacking. That was part one of her new plan. Tracy situated herself in the chair, and within seconds, she had logged in using the password she stole from Phil. Her first selection—Sleigh Routes.

When she opened the file, a little box popped up, asking whether she wanted text or graphics. She chose graphics and hit enter. A map of the world filled the screen, with the land divided into colored sections. Her own region—Florida, Georgia, and Atlanta—was purple. And within her region, there were several dozen colored lines criss-crossing the entire area.

At the bottom right corner of the screen was a button that said, "Mouse over for more information."

"I don't care what you think." That was Erlek. "You are coming with me, and so is that little nuisance."

The doorknob twisted, and Tracy froze, her heart pounding in her chest. Would they notice the screen if she turned around and blocked it with her body? She was about to do just that when she heard Beth's protest and Erlek's hand being yanked from the door handle.

"Ouch!" the elf cried.

"You will convince Walt to give us more time," said Beth, "or I'll tell him what you did last Thursday in toy storage."

"I didn't break *that* many toys."

"Five Leappads, two bicycles, and a Furby!"

"If you do that, I'll tell him about the time you..."

Tracy was still for a moment more, but when it seemed the argument was continuing, she sighed with relief and continued her task. She hovered the mouse over the Orlando area, and a text box appeared.

Name: Eugene Albert Blankenship

Region: East Orlando

Number of Houses: 708

Santa Command reloads: 5

So the guy who delivered presents to her house was named Eugene? Couldn't they have picked a guy who sounded more, well, Santa-y? Then again, if they were fooling the whole world, what did names matter? Santa was all about the look, and as long as the guy had the white beard and red suit, no one would know a thing. From what Phil and Beth had said, even Eugene didn't know it. His memory got wiped every Christmas.

Tracy's head hurt just thinking about that. She'd seen enough Star Trek to know that when people started messing with the mind, things got ugly. Did he forget other things too, like his wife's name, or his grandkid's birthday, or what he had for breakfast? Did they replace his memory with things that never happened, like a bad dream? And most importantly, did it hurt? It had to, considering Beth's reaction.

For the first time, Tracy realized she might not be safe after all. Beth seemed nice, and Phil seemed harmless, but they had a boss. And from what she'd heard, Walt wasn't a jolly guy in a red suit. He was someone to be afraid of.

"You have thirty seconds to get her or I'm calling Walt!" Erlek's voice boomed through the door.

"Oh no!" Tracy mumbled to herself. She moved the mouse to close the file, but instead of clicking the x in the corner, she moved her hand to her pocket instead. Her goal had been to find out the science behind Santa, and that hadn't changed. If she didn't get out in time, and they did manage to wipe her mind, she was going to need proof.

She pulled the turtle shaped zip drive from her pocket, plugged it into a slot on the computer, and started dragging files over to it. While the computer was transferring the third file, she got an error that said her drive was full.

"Oh no!" Tracy opened her drive, selected a bunch of files she'd downloaded at home from some video site, cut them from her drive, and moved them to the desk top. She was in such a hurry that her finger slipped, and she accidentally clicked one open. A string of numbers and letters filled the screen. She frowned. That certainly wasn't the TV show she downloaded. With no time to think about her messed up program, she closed it back up and started dragging files again.

The computer didn't like the next file. It was so big, a box appeared on the screen showing the slow, slow, slooow progress of the transfer. Tracy glanced toward the door. Phil, Beth, and the...creature were talking too low to hear again.

"Come on." Tracy drummed her nails on the desk, and then because she thought it couldn't hurt, she took a couple of other Santa files and dragged them over to her zip drive too, hoping they'd just queue up and save her a little time.

A loud buzz came from the computer. The hard drive whirred loudly, and the mouse froze in place on the screen.

"Uh oh!" Tracy tapped, then pounded on the keyboard. The whirring sound got louder and a bright red light came on inside the computer tower. She glanced toward the door, but thankfully no one else seemed to hear it. She tapped enter a few more times, and then *it* happened.

The blue screen of death.

Tracy bit off a scream as she read the words on the screen.

A problem has been detected and your operating system has been shut down to prevent damage to your computer. Beginning dump of physical memory.

And then a second later...

Dump of physical memory complete.

"No!" Tracy cried. "No! No! No! No!"

She pounded the keyboard, but nothing happened. The blue screen sat there, taunting her.

"Fine," Beth yelled from the hallway, "but you need to let us talk to her first!"

Then, the doorknob turned.

Tracy yanked her turtle out of the computer and enacted part two of her plan.

CHAPTER SIXTEEN

Santa Command—Main Frame
December 25th
0140 hours

Phil hovered behind Beth's shoulder as she opened the door. He had no idea what she was going to tell Tracy. This was about as bad as things could get.

But when the door was fully open, he saw the frozen computer. He also noticed that the girl was nowhere in sight, and he realized things were about to get a lot worse.

CHAPTER SEVENTEEN

Tracy

Tracy barely fit into the crawl space above the ceiling. When she first spotted the hatch, she assumed it was like her attic back home, large enough for her to walk through without ducking her head. Instead, Tracy found it difficult to even crawl. The floor was made up of narrow strips of plywood with nothing but the drywall of the ceiling and fluffy white insulation on either side of it. Tracy had no choice but to follow the path laid out by the boards. Because of the pipes and cables running across that path, she had to sometimes stretch out on her belly and wriggle herself through like a snake.

Also, it was very, very dark. She heard skittering all around her and wondered if she was hearing birds and squirrels, which would have been okay with her, or roaches and rats, which were not.

She was still wearing E. Higgens' coat. That made it harder to get through the tight spaces where she had to squeeze beneath the overhead support beams, but if she was going to escape, she was taking the coat as evidence. Maybe the computer files had finished uploading to her zip drive, maybe not, but she wasn't going home empty handed.

That was another problem, getting home. Her new plan involved getting to the loading bay and sneaking back on Santa's sleigh. She had gotten a good look at *her* Santa's picture on the computer and was sure she could figure out which one was him. His entire route was pretty close to her house. Ideally, she'd be able to get off close enough to walk home. If not, maybe she could call Ellen. She hadn't counted on Santa's crew being so uncooperative. Then again, she'd counted on Santa being real.

That was what made her head spin. For all of her life, heck, for all of her parents' and grandparents' lives, and on back for centuries, the Santa Commission had told them one thing above all else: that Santa was real.

But he wasn't. He was just some guy in a suit who never remembered a single Christmas Eve. He was worse than department store Santas. At least they knew the truth of what they were.

The dust in the crawl space tickled Tracy's nose.

She lifted her hand to her face and discovered that her cheeks were wet, and it wasn't from her outburst back in the computer room. She had set out to find the truth behind Santa. Where she'd expected to find rocket engines and fireproof clothing, she found instead something very different. And a lot more upsetting.

Who were Beth and Phil? What kind of people worked for someone who wiped minds? That wasn't science. It was science fiction. She half expected little robot elves with red eyes to come marching through the crawl space chanting, "You are mine! You are mine!"

At the very moment she pictured herself being carted off by an army of tiny robots, something skittered to her right, and she jumped. She squinted in the dark, but when the sound faded away and she realized no robots were coming for her, she breathed out a sigh of relief and moved on.

At least, she tried to. The hem of her coat caught on an exposed nail. She shoved her hand beneath her leg to unsnag herself, and as she adjusted her weight, the board beneath her slipped, and the nail scraped her thigh.

"Mmph!" She stifled a cry. Her leg throbbed in pain. How many ways could she injure herself in one night?

The answer came immediately as she rolled away from the nail, off of the board, and onto the ceiling. The drywall gave way beneath her, and she crashed down into a very strange room.

CHAPTER EIGHTEEN

Santa Command—Main Frame
December 25th
0200 hours

At that moment, Phil didn't care where Tracy was. He didn't care what she was doing. He didn't care what secrets she was learning. All he cared about was getting that computer back on line.

He quickly did the math in his head. The Alabama Command center was in charge of 187 different Santa routes. That was 160,000 houses! With two and a half hours to go, that meant there were still about 40,000 houses without presents. If he didn't get the Main Frame up immediately, they would fail. For the first time in the history of Santa Claus, the big guy would not complete his rounds.

First, Phil pulled the plug on the computer, hoping a simple restart would get everything going again. It did not. The blue screen returned and started flickering, almost like the computer was laughing at him.

Phil gripped the sides of the desk and let out an "Arggh!"

"You should have come with me when I asked." Erlek stood to the side grinning smugly. "Then you wouldn't be in this mess."

"Correction." Walt appeared in the doorway, his body a shadow against the brightly lit hallway. "You wouldn't be in this mess if you hadn't insisted on bringing that little girl here."

And now Walt's here, Phil thought. *Just great.* At least his boss couldn't do anything before he fixed the computer. Phil was the top programmer at Santa Command, and the only one who *could* fix it.

Walt stood blocking the door with his hands on his hips. "Every control room is at a standstill. We have no clue what people are seeing out there! It's our job to keep the secret. If we fail, what do you think my boss is going to do?"

Phil's blood pounded through his veins, and he wondered if he was going to have an early heart attack right then and there. He didn't worry so much about being fired, because he knew that was going to happen. He had joined Santa Command to help keep the secret, and that's what he was going to do. "I'm on it. Just give me a few minutes." He pulled a small spiral notebook and pen from his pocket and wrote down the error listed on the screen.

"Can I do anything?" Beth asked.

Phil sighed with a small amount of relief. At least there was one person who wasn't trying to send his blood pressure through the roof. In fact, there *was* something she could do, and Phil had the power to order it. "I need some more time."

"Time?" Beth asked like she wasn't sure she'd heard correctly. At Santa Command, that word carried a lot of weight.

"Do you have any idea what you're doing?" Walt asked.

"Yes." Phil answered both of them as he calculated what he thought he needed and not a second more. Still, he struggled with getting the words out of his mouth. Stopping time was tricky. It didn't always work out as planned, but at the moment, it was the only way. "I need half an hour."

Erlek blew out a low whistle. "Glad I'm not you."

Phil wanted to strangle the creature, but instead chose to focus on the computer screen. As Beth was leaving the room, Phil called back over his shoulder. "And do me a favor. Take the Inkling with you."

CHAPTER NINETEEN

Tracy

Tracy sneezed as the fluffy white insulation settled around her like snow. Well, at least something at Santa Command reminded her of the North Pole.

"Ouch," she said as she sat up and brushed dust out of her hair. Her tail bone was sore as well as her right arm. Again. She flexed her fingers. At least nothing was broken this time. She pushed herself off of the broken pieces of ceiling and to her feet.

She was in a square room, empty except for a large, oval shaped mirror mounted to the wall. The room had no windows, and the lights were out, but there was light coming from the mirror. It gave the room a soft, yellow glow like a living room lamp at night.

Tracy couldn't look away from the mirror, like it contained every happy memory in her life all rolled into one. She walked slowly toward it, even though the feeling in her bones told her to go for the door or find her way back to the attic. She needed to find out what the deal was with the mirror. Why did it glow like that? Why did she want to reach out and touch it?

As she got closer, the yellow light shivered, then swirled into an image, not a reflection, but a picture of a library. It was a lot like a trick she'd seen in Belle's house at Disney World, and she wondered if Santa Command had the same designers.

Once the picture stopped shifting, Tracy gaped at how welcoming everything looked. There was a red arm chair sitting next to a crackling fire. Green garland and red bows were draped across the mantle. The floor to ceiling bookshelves were stuffed with books. It was as if someone had reached into her mind and came up with the perfect reading room.

It was so detailed, she was certain she was looking through a window and not a mirror. But if the mirror was actually a door into another room, why not just build a door? Why go to the trouble of making it seem like a magical entrance when everything else in this building was fake? And why did her stomach feel so tingly when she looked at the mirror?

No, it wasn't tingles. She was just tired. The computer back in the other room had said it was around 2 am. No wonder the chair, with its fuzzy overstuffed cushions, looked so inviting.

But the presence of a comfy chair didn't explain why the room and the mirror were there in the first place. She knew in her gut the answer had to be important. *Think, Tracy, think. What does this room have to do with Santa Command?*

All of the people she had met seemed more interested in computers than in how their workplace looked. And if any of the Santas saw it, they wouldn't remember anyway. Besides, Tracy had the feeling the Santas weren't shown anything besides the dressing room and their sleighs. Get them in and out. Have them do their job, wipe their minds, then send them home, with stupid, fake memories.

Tracy had a crazy urge to step through the mirror just to feel what it was like in that library. It wasn't curiosity. It was more like a pull in the center of her body, tugging at her from the other room.

She put her hands on the sides of the frame in order to stop herself. She had other priorities—get to her Santa's sleigh and get home—but her body wasn't listening. Her breath came in quick little bursts. She tightened her fingers around the smooth wood. She shook her head, but instead of clearing her mind, her thoughts grew fuzzier.

One by one, her fingers let go of the frame, and her arms dropped loosely to her side. All on its own, her right foot stepped through the mirror, and the rest of her body had no choice but to follow.

CHAPTER TWENTY

Santa Command—Main Frame
December 25ᵗʰ
0205 hours

Phil's fingers flew across the keyboard. The entire Southeastern sector was frozen in time, Santas included. Fortunately, those inside Santa Command were immune to it, and he was able to work. He'd already restored the system. A virus had been uploaded to the computer, and he was pretty sure who had done it. His heart hammered wildly in his chest as he wondered how one little girl had managed to screw everything up so thoroughly.

Beth stood behind him and watched over his shoulder. She had come back to confirm that she'd gotten him the extra time. Erlek had not come back with her, and Walt had gone back to his office. Beth's presence, along with the others' absence, calmed him enough to focus on his task.

There were nine systems to reboot. He did the most critical ones first—sleigh power, navigation systems, and the Santa program. When those were done, and he had verified that all of the Santas were back on track, he activated the GPS in the Santa coats. That had been added a few years back as a security feature when one of the Santas fell out of his sleigh, and it had taken twenty-five minutes to find him. They'd stopped time that night too. Phil remembered with a shudder how close they'd come to disaster.

"Okay, I think we're good," Phil said. "Can you get time started again?"

Beth stepped out of the room, then returned a few moments later. "We're back."

As the GPS came on line, Phil watched the United States map on the screen light up with dozens of red, blinking dots, including his own sector. He exhaled with relief, hoping that he hadn't created another slew of problems.

Now, to find Tracy. He zoomed in on their area, focusing on Santa Command. Most of the dots in the building were motionless—those were the coats still hanging in the dressing room closets— but there was one dot moving through a room at the other end of Command.

Moving. Moving. And then it was gone.

Phil blinked, hoping his tired eyes were playing a trick on him. Of course he knew it wasn't a trick. There was only one room in Santa Command where Tracy could disappear like that, and no adult could follow her.

He slowly turned to Beth and saw the same panic on her face that he felt in his gut. That little girl had a knack of making the worst choice every single time. There was only person who could retrieve her now, and there was no guarantee that he'd be willing to try.

"Beth, I need you to make a phone call."

CHAPTER TWENTY-ONE

Jared

Jared lay in his bed, bouncing an orange foam ball against his bedroom door. He liked to do that when he couldn't sleep, and this time, Beth wouldn't be home until dawn to fuss at him.

She had called several times, but thankfully, she stopped just after midnight. No, wait. He thought too soon, because her ring tone blasted out of his phone. It was lodged somewhere in the pile of dirty clothes at the bottom of his closet, where he had been ignoring it all night. She could talk to his voice mail. Maybe he could change the message to state that he was eleven and far too old to have her checking on him every hour.

While his phone rang and beeped, he bounced the orange ball against his door forty six times. But then, he missed the ball, so he had to get up anyway and decided to find his phone, just so he could shut it off.

He dug through his clothes, tossing shirts and sweaters behind him until his fingers touched something hard and plastic. He fished it out of the pile, then realized it wasn't his phone. It was a CD. His stomach twisted when he saw it. He'd buried it for a reason, but he hadn't buried it deep enough.

His phone trumpeted with a text, but he barely heard it. The memory of a long ago Saturday afternoon filled his mind. His dad had popped the CD in his stereo, proclaiming that it was time to introduce Jared to the best band in the world. From the very first chord, his dad sang loudly and jumped around the living room playing air guitar while Jared rolled his eyes and complained. His dad, enjoying himself too much to stop, patted Jared on the shoulder and proclaimed, "One day, son, you'll cherish memories like this."

"Not likely," Jared said back then.

And not now either. He blinked, willing the memory to vanish. Of all of the Christmas gifts he had ever received, this one had been the cruelest. He spied his trashcan across the room. It would be so easy to just throw the CD away. Could he do it?

Another text came through, and he dropped the CD, like it had burned him. His phone lit up among the pile of clothes.

We need your help. Can you come? Please?

Ordinarily, he would have ignored Beth's request.

He didn't want anything to do with Santa Command, but tonight, he couldn't sit in his room anymore, not with that CD staring at him.

He picked up his phone and texted back.

I'm on my way.

CHAPTER TWENTY-TWO

Tracy

The moment Tracy stepped into the library, she felt warmth spread through her body, like she had walked into a dream. She wanted to curl up in the chair, dangle her toes near the fire, and settle in with a long book.

Once again, Tracy wondered what this room was doing at Santa Command. Did they use it to train the Santas how to get up and down chimneys? That was another item on her list she needed to figure out for her project. As quickly as the thought entered her mind, it was gone, replaced with the sweet smell of cinnamon coming from a plate of cookies on a small table between the chair and fireplace.

She realized how hungry she was and took one. As the Snickerdoodle melted in her mouth, she sank down into the comfy chair and lazily picked up a book from a stack on the table. She traced her fingers over the maroon and gold cover, then flipped through the crinkly, yellowed pages. The words were handwritten in fancy cursive, and some of the letters didn't look right, but Tracy didn't have to read it all to know what it said. She had memorized the poem long ago—'*Twas the Night Before Christmas*.

Her father recited it every year on Christmas Eve just before they all went to bed. She always chimed in, reciting her favorite parts with him.

The watercolor drawings in the book were comfortingly familiar. The dad in the stocking cap had black hair and thick eyebrows just like her father. The fireplace had one red stocking and two green ones just like at her house. There was even a long brown sofa like the one she slept on when she was eight years old, hoping to get a glimpse of Santa.

"Weird," Tracy said.

She pulled her feet up under her and reached for the cup of hot chocolate that was sitting on the table. She didn't remember it being there before, but figured she must have missed it. It had mini marshmallows floating in it and a cinnamon stick for stirring, just like her mom always made it. She gulped the drink down, then set the cup on the table and curled up into a ball with the book clutched to her chest and her eyes closed.

As she drifted to sleep, she thought less about her science project and Santa Command and more about the feeling the library gave her, that she was home and safe and happy.

Her dream started with her living room and the brown couch and the fishing line tied around her finger. It was Christmas Eve, and she was waiting for Santa to slide down the chimney. She was lying on the couch with her eyes closed, but was too anxious for sleep. Every time she heard a noise, she would peek at the fireplace with one eye. It wasn't until the house grew completely silent that he showed up.

"I'm here, Tracy," came a soft, low voice from across the room.

She sat up and rubbed her eyes. "Santa? I've been looking for you."

He laughed in that merry way of his. His belly even shook. It made Tracy smile to see that he was just like the poem described him. "I see that. What can I do for you?"

"I need...something." But she couldn't remember what. She knew it wasn't a toy or a book or a doll. It was something much more important.

"Did you send me a letter?"

"No, I don't think I did." Tiny memories tugged at the corners of her mind, but they wouldn't form a complete thought. "A letter wasn't enough. It wouldn't work."

Santa sat down on the sofa beside Tracy and sighed. "I get that a lot. Some kids have wishes, others have troubles."

"Yeah. A trouble, and I need you to fix it."

Santa wrapped his large, weathered hand around Tracy's small one. "You know," he said in a way that made him seem very wise and very weary, "there are some troubles that even I can't fix."

"I know that, but I'm pretty sure you weren't the one that was supposed to fix it." Tracy shook her head. It was like she had a hundred different puzzle pieces floating around in her mind, but they were from a bunch of different puzzles, so only a few pieces matched up. "It was something *I* had to do, but it had everything to do with you."

"Are you sure you don't need me? Sometimes, plans have to be modified."

Tracy looked up into Santa's soft blue eyes, and was comforted by what she saw. Centuries of kindness and wisdom had been etched into his very core. This was Santa. Maybe he did hold the answer to her problem. She just had to figure out what the problem was.

She rubbed her fist across her eyes. "I should go back to sleep," she said. Maybe her brain wouldn't feel so muddled in the morning. "Will I be able to find you when I wake up?"

"Most people wouldn't be able to, but I'll bet

you're a little different than most."

"Thank you." Tracy laid her head on a fuzzy green throw pillow and as she drifted back to sleep, she heard Santa shuffling around in the living room, doing his job as only he could.

Tracy didn't know how long she slept. There could have been other dreams, but they were the unimportant kind, usually filled with talking spatulas and shifting landscapes. The dream about Santa sneaked through, his words stuck in her brain as if he had stitched them there.

Sometimes, plans have to be modified.

"Tracy?" A popping sound came from nearby. "Hello?"

Tracy rubbed the sleep out of her eyes, then blinked. Standing before her was a boy about her age. He was bigger than her though, like he might be a football player in a year or two. His hair was cut in a short, blonde buzz cut, and his head was tilted like he'd been calling her name for a while.

He snapped his thick fingers in front of her eyes, confirming her thoughts.

She pushed his hand out of the way and sat up straight in the chair. "Who are you?" she asked.

"I'm Jared," he said in a tired voice that sounded like he had been dragged out of bed. "Beth sent me to get you."

CHAPTER TWENTY-THREE

Santa Command—Portal Room
December 25ᵗʰ
0225 hours

Phil stared at the portal with his arms folded across his chest and his face pinched into a frown.

Beth nudged her shoulder against his. "Didn't anyone ever tell you your face will freeze like that?"

He knew that she was only trying to get him to relax, but the way she said it, super fast, blending all the words together, only stressed him out more.

He glanced at the time on his phone. "Jared's been gone for five minutes. Shouldn't they be back now?" He was afraid that if Tracy stayed too long, she would run into something interesting. And by "interesting" he meant something Tracy shouldn't be seeing at all.

Jared was different. When he went to live with Beth, she told him everything about Santa Command in order to gain his trust, but Jared didn't believe her. In fact, Phil and Beth had lied to him about why they needed him to go get Tracy, because for Jared, the lie was easier to believe than the truth. The kid had created his own reality about Santa Command, and no one could convince him otherwise. He would never tell anyone their secrets, because he thought he'd sound like an idiot.

Tracy, on the other hand, was dangerous. He could see that now. She didn't try to hack their main frame out of pure curiosity. She planned to tell someone. When she got back, Phil knew what he had to do. "Just wait a few more minutes," Beth said. Again, it was like her voice was being played in fast forward.

"Why are you talking like that?" Now it wasn't just her voice. He sounded like a recording of Alvin and the Chipmunks. What was going on? It was like time itself were malfunctioning. That couldn't be happening. Could it?

He reached for his phone again, but before he could check it, the ground rumbled beneath them, and the room lurched. He grabbed hold of Beth's arm as the two of them stumbled.

"Whoa!" she said. "Was that an earthquake?"

"I don't think it—"

His statement got swallowed up by another shift that knocked both of them to their knees. When Phil looked up a second later, he wished it had been an earthquake.

The portal was gone. The connection was severed.

Did that mean...?

He punched in a number on his phone, which should have connected him to the command center in Virginia. It didn't ring or go to voice mail, and his fears were confirmed.

They'd been knocked out of time. Their entire sector, three states, thirty four million people, was disconnected from the rest of the world.

CHAPTER TWENTY-FOUR

Tracy

"To *get* me?" Tracy asked warily. "And where do you plan to take me?"

"Home," Jared said.

"I get to go home? Just like that?"

He shrugged.

"But I thought they were going to take me—" Tracy bit off the word. What if this was just a trick to get her to come along quietly? Last she heard, they were taking her to Walt to wipe her mind. "I don't believe you."

"Look, I don't care if you don't believe me," Jared sounded bored, "but my aunt said to tell you that she'll protect you. I think they're gonna sneak you out or something."

"Who's your aunt?"

"Beth."

"Oh." Tracy still wasn't sure she believed him, but she believed that Beth didn't want to hurt her. She had stood up for Tracy in the computer room. Besides, Tracy had to get out of the library. She didn't like the tingly feeling in her stomach, and she didn't like that she'd fallen asleep and almost forgotten her plans.

"All right," she said to Jared. "Let's go." At the first sign of a lie, she'd figure out a way to ditch him.

"Fine." Jared walked to the door/mirror, but stopped right in front of it. It didn't have that yellow glow anymore.

Jared touched it, and...nothing happened. It didn't shiver or swirl or look anything like it did before. It was just a mirror, a lot like the one in Tracy's bathroom.

She watched Jared's reflection as he leaned in close and squinted, like he was trying to see through it to the other side. His face was round and scrunched up like a cartoon character. He tapped the mirror a couple more times, then he took a step back, crossed his arms across his chest, and frowned. "Huh."

Tracy stepped up beside the mirror, put her fingers under one of the side edges, and lifted. Maybe a real mirror had slid into place, covering the doorway. When she peered behind the mirror, all she saw was a blank wall. She even slid her hand behind the mirror to feel the wall, thinking it could be another illusion. It wasn't. The wall was as solid as the mirror. That left her with only one logical conclusion.

She turned to Jared with her hands on her hips and a nasty look on her face. "What's going on here? This isn't the same room I went to sleep in. You must have carried me here while I was sleeping." He was big enough.

Jared put his hands on his hips in a perfect imitation of her and snapped right back. "I didn't do anything. I came through that mirror, same as you. Maybe it broke when you looked at it."

The insult made Tracy turn her back to him and huff. Clearly, this boy had no intention of helping her get home. "Fine. If you're going to be that way, I'll find my own way home." She headed for the actual door, which was on the far side of the room, to the left of the fireplace.

Jared laughed as she opened the door. "Good luck with that."

Tracy stepped through and gave him a snotty little wave.

He crossed the room like he was going to stop her. "Just see if you can find your way without—" His words cut off when Tracy shut the door in his face.

CHAPTER TWENTY-FIVE

Tracy

Tracy stepped into a hallway that had no trace of the plain white walls and fluorescent lighting she had seen in the rest of Santa Command. It was dark and felt more like she was visiting someone's home. Candlelight from the wall sconces gave her enough light to see that the hallway seemed to go on forever. Every square inch of the walls was covered with framed photographs of children on Christmas morning: little girls with baby doll carriages, little boys dressed as cowboys, riding pretend ponies, wide eyed toddlers getting their first view of the presents Santa left, and much more. They were all black and white, some so old and faded, she could barely make out the details. But as she walked down the hall, the pictures grew more recent. She saw color photos of kids holding up big chunky video games like her parents played when they were little, then kids sorting through stacks of CDs, and most recently, kids absorbed in their iPhones and iPads.

She ran her finger across some of the photos, recognizing many of the toys that she had owned when she was smaller. Her finger stopped on one picture in particular. Tracy's mouth dried out as she gaped at the picture of her and Pim taken on the night before Pim's accident. It was Christmas Eve. The two girls had their arms around each other, and they were wearing the matching footie pajamas they had been given—red for Tracy, blue for Pim.

Tracy remembered the night vividly. They were both missing a couple of teeth, and the two of them sang All I Want for Christmas is My Two Front Teeth about a hundred times that day. After the accident, Tracy had visited Pim in the hospital and played that song for hours, over and over hoping her cousin would recognize it and talk, or blink, or do something. It never happened and when nighttime came, her parents made her go home. Tracy hadn't been able to listen to that song since without crying.

Tracy pulled her finger from the picture and wiped the tear from her cheek. That's why she had hopped in Santa's sleigh. That's why she needed him. How could she have forgotten such an important thing? And how had she even dreamed of going home without her evidence?

She couldn't let Pim down. She had to win that prize money, and the Santa coat she was wearing wasn't going to be enough.

Tracy wiped one final tear from her cheek and straightened her shoulders. She was going to get the information she needed, and no one was going to stop her.

"Hello, there."

The voice came from behind her. Tracy whirled around to see a tiny, gray-haired man standing there. He was chubby, wearing a navy blue vest, jacket and dress pants, and barely taller than Tracy herself.

"Where did you come from?" Tracy asked. There hadn't been any other doors in the hallway, except for the one she came through.

The man pointed to a door about two feet away.

Tracy blinked several times. "I didn't see that door before."

"Sometimes," he said gently, "things exist whether you see them or not. You were looking pretty intently at that picture. Do you want to tell me about it?"

"No." What she wanted was to get moving, but she had to get around this guy first. "Who are you?"

"Hmm." He scratched his stubbly chin while he thought about the answer. "I could tell you, but you wouldn't believe me, so I don't think I'll bother for now."

"Try me. I doubt this night could get any weirder."

The man smiled. A twinkle sat in the corner of his eye. "Oh, I assure you, it can. One person's weird is another person's calling."

"Huh?" Tracy didn't have time for riddles. She glanced down the hall to see if she could find an end to it or another doorway.

"In a hurry, are you?"

"I suppose you're going to ask me to come with you? I'm tired of hearing that, so if you'll just let me go, I'll—"

"Go ahead." He stretched his arm to point down the hallway. His door was gone, and once again, she saw nothing but pictures lining the walls.

A banging sound echoed from behind them, followed by a muffled voice shouting, "Hey! Hey, where did you go?" Tracy was pretty sure it was Jared, back in the library.

The man noticed it too and turned in that direction. "Well, if you'll excuse me, I think I'll go check on your friend. He seems worried." And he walked away.

Tracy couldn't believe he was just going to leave her there. "Hey!"

The man kept walking toward Jared, but waggled his fingers over his shoulder. "Carry on. My house is yours."

Tracy looked down the hallway to see if any more

doors popped open. At that point she would have believed it, but nothing happened. If anything, the hall seemed to stretch longer, as if it really did go on forever.

She started walking away from the man. She ran her fingers around the pictures, looking for hidden seams in the walls. She knocked on random patches to see if she heard a hollow sound, like a room was on the other side. The less she found, the faster she walked. Nothing, nothing, and more nothing. Just thousands of pictures, with no end in sight. She ran, trying to find any way out, but when her breath gave out, she stopped and turned around. The man was no further away from her than he was before. She could still hear Jared hollering from the other side of the library door, and the man was still walking toward him. Tracy's shoulders slumped. Her options had run out. "Wait for me!" she called.

The man stopped, looked over his shoulder, and smiled.

CHAPTER TWENTY-SIX

Tracy

"Help! Lemme out of here! Help!" Jared's muffled cries were emphasized by his fists pounding on the door. "Who locked the—"

The man turned the shiny brass knob, and when he opened the door, Jared fell through and spilled to the ground in front of Tracy's feet.

"— door?" Jared finished quietly. He stood up and brushed himself off, trying to restore whatever dignity he'd lost by falling. "Um, hey, Chris."

"Jared." Chris smiled like the two were old friends. "How is your aunt?"

"Good. She's good. Um, I was just..." He nodded toward Tracy.

"Ah, yes. You're here for Miss Tam?"

Miss Tam? Tracy hadn't told him her first name, much less her last. "Hey, how did you—?"

"How do we get back?" Jared seemed irritated, just like he had back in the library. Apparently, he had no other emotions. "The door is gone. Is that room on a turntable or something?"

"Hmm." Chris pressed his lips into a fine line. "That's one explanation."

Jared bounced back and forth from one foot to the other. He was so big, he should have looked clumsy, but it almost looked like he was dancing. "Can you turn the room back to where it was so we can get going?"

Chris stuck his head just inside the room, looked around, then came back out. "No."

"No?" Jared whined. "Beth is gonna kill me if I don't bring her back."

"The portal disconnected. It looks like tonight is turning out to be quite interesting."

"Portal?" Tracy asked. "What are you talking about? We want the door."

Chris patted her shoulder with a sad look on his face. "Don't worry. You'll understand before the night is over."

"But the door?" Jared asked.

"In time," Chris said. With that, he turned on his heel and marched back down the hallway. After about five steps, he snapped his fingers and a door opened to his right side. He stepped through, then leaned his head back out to call out to Tracy and Jared. "Well, come on you two. The night is fading fast. We have lots to cover." He let out a deep, rich laugh, then disappeared through the door.

Tracy and Jared looked at each other and shrugged. What else could they do but follow him?

***

They found themselves outside, standing in snow about six inches deep. Wind whipped through the surrounding forest. Both Tracy and Jared shivered, but he wasn't lucky enough to be wearing a Santa coat. All he had on was a sweatshirt and jeans. Tracy felt sorry for him as he scrubbed his sleeve across his watery eyes and wrapped his arms around his middle. Her sorrow was short-lived though as the snow began seeping in around the edges of her thin canvas sneakers. It took exactly five seconds for her feet to become frozen popsicles.

"Where are we?" Tracy quietly asked Jared while Chris marched on ahead of them.

"Same place you've been all night." Jared kicked at a mound of snow. The powder flew through the air and blew back against Tracy's legs. "Nothing here is real. I'm sure there's a snow machine hidden somewhere and about a hundred mirrors."

Tracy murmured her agreement while looking

around to see if she could spot where any of them were hidden. She stuck her hand in her pocket to make sure the camera was still there.

Jared blew into his hands and rubbed them together. His skin had turned pink from the cold. "Why are you here anyway? My aunt called me in the middle of the night to come get you because she had to get back to her job. It's your fault we're stuck following him."

Chris called to them without looking back. "My dear Jared, please don't blame Tracy for things you don't understand."

Tracy and Jared exchanged a glance.

"How did he hear us?" Tracy silently mouthed the words.

Jared shrugged. Clearly, he was done speaking to her.

Chris turned around and waited until the two kids caught up. "You'll find I know a great many things that defy explanation. My wife is constantly baffled. She has a scientific mind like you, Tracy."

Tracy smiled. It was something she was very proud of. But how did he know that?

He must have seen the question in her eyes, because he said, "My wife learned to believe, and one day, so will you." He waggled his eyebrows, and the stars danced in his eyes. "Maybe even tonight." He turned back around, and suddenly, the three of them were standing in front of a large, red barn that hadn't been there a moment ago. "Ah!" He clapped his hands and rubbed them together with excitement. "Here we are."

CHAPTER TWENTY-SEVEN

Tracy

Chris cracked open the large barn door. It swung out over the snow, and the three of them stepped up into the barn. The inside was pitch black. Chris's footsteps echoed as he disappeared into the darkness.

Tracy hovered near the door. Jared leaned back against the wall with his arms folded. He looked comfortable, like he spent a lot of time in that position.

She wanted to ask him questions, like how he knew Chris and what the heck was going on, but she didn't feel like getting snapped at by him again. If he wasn't talking to her, then she wasn't talking to him.

"Don't worry, my friends." Chris reappeared with a large candle and lit it with a match from inside his coat pocket. He held up the light near his face, but instead of looking freaky like most people did when they held a flashlight up under their chin, he looked kind. He smiled, and his cheeks showed off tiny dimples. "You'll understand soon enough. This way," he said, as he headed into the barn's shadows.

Tracy followed first with Jared close behind her. If she had learned anything since meeting Chris, it was that she had to follow him or be left behind. And if she got left behind, she was lost. More importantly, she wanted to follow him. The more time she spent with the old man, the more she felt drawn to him, like she had a magnet inside of her pulling her to him. It made no sense, but things had stopped making sense the moment she crept out of her house and onto Santa's sleigh.

They passed several empty animal stalls. One had a worn out board hanging half way off the door. Tracy could just make out the letters "ond" engraved into it. She wondered what happened to Pond, the name she made up for him in her head. The barn smelled like a cold, icy night, with no hay or manure scents anywhere. Whatever happened to him, it was a long time ago.

Chris paid no attention to the stalls, instead heading toward a dark lump in the back of the barn. As they got closer, Tracy realized the lump was a burlap cloth, which covered something roughly the size of her dad's Toyota.

"Help me, will you?" Chris set his candle on the floor and grabbed an edge of the cloth.

Tracy and Jared did the same, and together, the three of them pulled. As the cloth dropped to the ground, decades of dust puffed into the air. Tracy waved her hand in front of her face. Jared took a step back and coughed. Chris just stood there and smiled like he was seeing a long lost friend.

"You wanted us to see a sleigh?" Tracy asked.

Chris didn't answer. He was too wrapped up in his treasure. The outside of the sleigh was red with gold trim, but even in the faint light, Tracy could tell it had seen a lot of years. It was covered with scuffs and scratches, the kind that made it seem well-loved. Chris stepped over the bunched up cloth and slowly climbed into the sleigh. He took hold of the reins, which were still draped across the front, and sat up tall. His face seemed to glow, as if light were bursting from within him and not coming from the single candle still sitting on the floor.

His enthusiasm was contagious. Tracy bounced on the balls of her feet.

"Well, what are you waiting for?" Chris called to the children. "Hop in!"

Tracy was waiting for his invitation and jumped right in, unable to wait a second longer.

Jared shrugged again, like he was doing his best to stay grumpy, but he climbed in anyway.

The sleigh was much older than the one Tracy had

been in just a few hours before. The seat was wooden and worn to a smooth finish. The space for Santa's bags was much smaller and would never have fit Tracy and the pile of bags she'd been crammed in with earlier.

"So," Tracy asked, "did you used to be one of the Santas?" Based on the dust tickling her nose, he wasn't anymore.

Chris laughed his deep laugh again. Tracy smiled when she heard it. "Not *one* of the Santas. *The* Santa. The original."

Tracy's smile switched into a frown. "What do you mean? There is no real Santa. It's just a bunch of guys playing dress up, and they don't even know about it." She looked to Jared to confirm it. He was Beth's nephew, and he obviously knew about Santa Command, so he would agree with her at least on that point.

"Dress up?" Jared snorted. "Zombie Santa is more like it."

Tracy had to agree. "They are kind of creepy, aren't they?"

"I'm sorry," Chris said gently as he smoothed the reins across his lap. "I wish things could be different."

"I'm sorry too. I wish you were the real Santa." Jared looked up. "I used to think so. Beth told me you were. But, I know the truth now. I mean, you'd have to be thousands of years old, and you'd have to have real magic, not all those tricks they use at Santa Command."

"Oh, I see." Chris said quietly. "You need to see real magic."

Tracy snorted.

"Real magic doesn't exist," Jared said.

"Hm, I thought you would say as much." Chris turned to Tracy who sat on the opposite side of him. "I suppose your laugh means you agree with Jared?"

Tracy gave a firm nod. "Everything in this world has a scientific explanation. That's why I came to Santa Command to begin with. I needed to—" Tracy stopped and looked at the wall. She had no idea what Chris would say about her plan, and now wasn't the time to find out.

"You needed to...what?" Chris urged her.

"I..." Tracy pulled at the cuffs of her Santa coat. "I needed to see for myself how everything worked."

"Well, I can see that this is going to be an interesting night, for all of us."

"Why's that?" Tracy asked.

Chris' eyes twinkled again as he snapped the reins. "Hang on." Slowly, the sleigh lifted off the ground.

Tracy grabbed onto the edge as the sleigh wobbled in the air. A moment later, Tracy was glad she was holding onto something, because the sleigh made a sharp turn to the left, wobbled once more, then shot out through the barn door and up into the night sky.

CHAPTER TWENTY-EIGHT

Tracy

The frozen world fell away beneath them as they rose up, up, up into the sky. The cold air stole Tracy's breath, and at one point, she swore she was so high she could touch the moon. She reached her hand up just in case, but when Chris looked at her from the corner of his eye, she felt self-conscious and dropped her hand back into her lap.

"Ha ha!" Chris bellowed joyfully and jerked the reins. They zoomed off above the trees.

There were no fake reindeer in front of them, but Chris manipulated the reins as if there were. When the sleigh twisted to the left, Tracy slid into Chris's side. When it twisted to the right, Tracy got squished between him and the side of the sleigh. Her whole body tingled, just like it had when she was five and had ridden that spinny ride at the fair with Pim. The two of them must have ridden it a dozen times, trying to squish each other into pancakes. But this was even better.

The world was silent and perfect, the way Tracy always imagined Christmas night should be. She didn't care if it was mirrors or video screens or some high tech Disney-type trick. It was Christmas, and up there in the sky, everything felt right.

The moon reflected on the snow and made it look like the ground was covered in diamonds. She wanted to roll around in it and fill the landscape with snow angels. They soared over trees solid white with ice, and Tracy thought she had entered some sort of fairy tale. She could have never imagined anything so beautiful if she had tried. Even more amazing were the colored lights filling the sky. It was like a rainbow had turned into a river.

"What's that?" she asked.

"The Northern Lights," Chris said. "I like to think the heavens create them just for me on this night."

Tracy understood. She felt as if the night was putting on a show just for her. Even in the bitter cold, she felt warm on the inside. Her troubles had been nestled deep inside of her for so long, but as they flew, those troubles seemed to loosen and break free. Riding in that sleigh, life seemed more possible. Jared, however, didn't seem amazed at all, just tired.

"Look over the side, just ahead," Chris said.

The two children poked their faces over the edge. "Polar bears," Tracy exclaimed. "A mom and two babies!"

The baby bears flopped around in the snow, giving themselves a bath. When they were done with that, they used their mother as a jungle gym. Tracy watched until she could no longer see them, then settled back into the seat.

"They're always twins, you know," Jared said from the other side of Chris.

Tracy peeked around Chris and saw Jared looking at her. It was the first time he seemed excited about anything.

"I'm gonna be a biologist when I grow up," he explained. "Probably for marine mammals."

Tracy wrinkled her nose at the thought of working around animals all the time. She'd been to Sea World. She knew what the seal and dolphin tanks smelled like. Still, Tracy felt a certain kinship with him that she hadn't before. "I like science too. I want to work in a lab though, developing medicine."

"You know," Chris said, "science is its own kind of magic."

"Not this again." Jared rolled his eyes and turned away so he was looking off at the distant mountains.

Tracy didn't argue. She actually agreed with Chris.

Something had changed while they were up in the air. If someone had asked why she was ready to talk, she would have said the twinkle in Chris' eye gave her a pinprick of hope. "I know someone who needs that type of magic. Very badly."

"Oh?" Chris laid the reins across his lap and turned to Tracy. The sleigh didn't seem to mind. It stayed on course without so much as a wiggle. It looked old-fashioned, but must have been fitted with jet engines just like the other sleighs. "Would you like to tell me about her?"

Tracy narrowed her eyes. "How did you know it was a her?"

"The girl in the picture."

Of course. He'd seen her crying over the picture in the hallway. "My cousin Pim. She fell out of a tree two years ago, and her brain doesn't work right anymore. She's awake and can say a word or two, but she's not... right. She can't go to school. She can't even play video games with me."

"Oh, dear," Chris said.

She had Jared's attention too. He was staring at her with his mouth hanging open. Tracy wished he wasn't. She didn't want his pity.

"Anyway," she continued, looking only at Chris, "my aunt found out about this operation they think will fix her, but it's really expensive."

"I see." For the first time that night, Chris looked sad. His mouth turned down at the edges, and his eyes lost their glow.

"Yeah, so I had this plan to get the money...a state science fair."

Jared's eyes perked up at the mention of the science fair.

Tracy glared at him. "*I'm* going to win it. Pim needs that operation."

"Well, I need a new Xbox, but it doesn't matter. Beth told me you live in Florida. I don't."

"Oh." Tracy hadn't thought about that. "So anyway, I had the perfect project. It just hasn't turned out as well as I thought it would."

"And what is your project?" Chris asked softly.

"It's...um..." What was she supposed to tell him? She had sneaked onto Santa's sleigh, cut a hole in his bag, and took pictures and video that she was pretty sure no one in the world was supposed to see. That had all been part of her plan, and she might have confessed right away if that was all she had done. Unfortunately, her plan had fallen completely apart, and she'd been forced to improvise. It had all been in the name of helping Pim, but the more she thought about it, the more her stomach started to hurt. It twisted in knots like the time she had worn her mom's bracelet to school without permission, and then lost it on the playground. Tracy hadn't touched her dinner that night, and at three am the next morning, she got up and confessed to her mom. Her mom took away her allowance for a month, but Tracy didn't mind, because the pain was gone.

Tracy clutched her stomach as she realized what exactly was making it hurt now, and it was far worse than a lost bracelet. In the past few hours, she had snatched one of the Santa coats with the intention of keeping it, stolen a camera from another child, and broken Santa Command's main computer. And after all of that, she ran away. Were Phil and Beth even able to fix the computer? How many kids were going to miss Christmas because of her? The Santas may have been fake, but the presents and the spirit of giving were not. That was something Tracy had forgotten, but her stomach was doing a very good job of reminding her. As her stomach twisted in on itself, Tracy realized it was time to make the pain go away.

"Chris?"

"Yes, Tracy?"

"I think I've done something very bad."

CHAPTER TWENTY-NINE

Tracy

The excitement from the ride disappeared. She wanted nothing more than to be on the ground where she could pace or call someone or do something.

She grabbed hold of Chris' arm. "I need to go back to Santa Command. I need to talk to Phil or Beth. I've got to fix this."

"Fix what?" Jared asked. "What did you do?"

How could she explain the importance of it all? How could she justify what she had done? "I was trying to do a good thing. I wanted to get Pim back. My whole family needs her back."

"Will you tell me?" Chris watched her with wide, concerned eyes. For some reason, she didn't want to disappoint him, but she didn't have another choice.

She took a deep breath and blurted out, "I broke Christmas."

Chris didn't scowl or reprimand her. He didn't even ask her to explain. He simply waved his hand in the air. A trail of yellow stars dropped from his palm, and the three of them were back in the barn, sleigh and all.

"Whoa!" Jared said. He jumped to the floor and tapped the walls of the barn. "Did you have theme park engineers install that ride?"

Chris took a curvy, black pipe out of his vest pocket, lit it, took a few puffs, and leaned back in the sleigh. "My dear boy, I have no idea what you're talking about."

The candle that Chris had left on the floor was still burning. The light flickered on the barn walls. Jared moved into the shadows, but Tracy could see him poking each knothole that he came to. When that didn't give him any results, he ran into one of the stalls behind the sleigh. Tracy couldn't see him anymore, but his breath sounded wobbly like he was trying to climb something. "Where are the projectors? There has to be a bunch of them to accomplish something like this. I couldn't even tell we were looking at a screen."

Tracy turned around in her seat and saw that Jared was now standing on his tiptoes on the half wall between two stalls and sticking his hands into every crack and crevice he could find.

"I saw this special on Discovery Channel," he said, "that talked about theme park rides and how they did

Spiderman and Harry Potter at Universal. Is that how you did this? Is it built on the same type of platform?"

Chris didn't watch Jared. He just smoked his pipe and laughed. He clearly enjoyed the boy's questions.

Tracy didn't. Jared had gone from rude to hyper in a matter of seconds, and neither one was any help. She hopped out of the sleigh and fussed at him. "Will you stop wasting time? There's maybe three hours left before the sun comes up."

Jared jumped from the wall and landed agilely on his feet in front of Tracy. His eyes nearly popped out of their sockets, making him look less like a future football player and more like a cartoon character. "Are you kidding? We just went on the most amazing ride ever. Don't you want to know how he did it?"

"No, I don't." She folded her arms across her chest, which was kind of hard, because the Santa coat bunched up in weird places. "I told you. We have a huge problem to fix. Don't you care?"

"Nope," he said bluntly. "My aunt works at Santa Command. If the old man misses my house, she'll still bring my presents home. Besides, you didn't look too worried when you were passed out in Chris' library. When did you start caring?"

"When we…" Well, the truth was, she didn't know exactly what had made her change her mind, but it had been sometime after she had stepped through that mirror. She didn't care if there were jets on the sleigh or if it had all been a ride. "It doesn't matter. At least I care about something more than getting my presents."

"That's not what I—"

Chris hopped down from the sleigh and landed in between the children. "How about we go inside and warm up?" he said as he rubbed his hands together briskly. "My wife makes a mean cup of hot chocolate."

"But—" Tracy began.

"Patience." Chris put a finger to her lips. "I promise you, we'll take care of your problem, but there's something else that needs to be done first." And with that, Chris turned on his heel and walked out of the barn. The two children followed behind, but they refused to look at each other for the entire walk.

***

Chris' wife, he introduced her as Mary, placed four steaming mugs of hot chocolate on the tiny breakfast table in the corner of the kitchen. It tasted just like the one Tracy had found in the library, sweet and spicy, and Tracy settled back into her chair.

Mary looked like an older version of a 1950s housewife, with a puffy skirt, lacy apron, and wavy, gray hair. Both the kitchen and her appearance showed that she liked things neat and orderly. Tracy could appreciate that. She couldn't sleep if her desk had a pencil out of place.

Mary's kitchen smelled like the Main Street bakery at Disney. Her parents had told her that Disney piped in that smell to sell more cookies, but Tracy had a feeling the scent in Mary's kitchen was the real thing. It was odd to think anything about her night was real, when she had found so many things that made her question what she knew. That was the very nature of science, to raise questions and seek answers, no matter how unexpected those answers might be. She stuck her hand inside her coat pocket and felt the turtle zip drive.

Despite the confusing answers she'd gotten, she still had so many questions. What were those elf creatures? Where did she go when she went through that mirror? She didn't feel like they were in Alabama anymore. Was it really a portal? Did Santa Command have transporter technology like on Star Trek? And last of all, who was Chris? Of everything she had discovered, he felt the most real, but she still didn't know what that meant. He said he was the original Santa. She agreed with Jared on that one. It wasn't possible.

She studied Chris across the table. He had red cheeks and dimples, no beard, just some scruff, but whiskers come and go. If she tilted her head and squinted her eyes just a little bit, she could sort of see how he looked like Santa.

Chris noticed Tracy studying him. He wiggled his fingers, and for a moment, he transformed into Tracy's perfect image of Santa—red suit, fat belly, warm smile—but a second later, he was back in his navy blue suit, looking very much like a retired business man.

Jared noticed it too and spit his hot chocolate all over the table. "I knew this stuff was tainted!"

"Jared!" Mary scolded him as she handed him a wet washcloth to clean up his mess. Her hair was neat and her back was straight, and she was not the type to clean up after children who were perfectly capable of doing it themselves.

Chris laughed it off. "It's all right, my dear. It'll wash."

Mary raised an eyebrow.

Tracy pulled her cup closer to her and swished it around. Was that what had changed her mind? The drink in the library? *No, it wasn't,* said a voice inside her, although it didn't tell her why. She set her cup down before it sloshed out and she also got on Mary's bad side.

Jared finished mopping up his mess, then plopped back down in his seat. He pushed his mug to the center of the table. When Mary glared at him, he said, "I'm done, thank you."

She wasn't so easily satisfied. "Jared Astor, when have I ever served you a tainted drink?"

He scoffed. "Probably always."

Mary opened her mouth to argue, but Chris put his hand on hers. "My dear, I believe Jared has been going through a tough time. Perhaps we should allow him to speak."

When he put it that way, she couldn't very well say no. She gave him a curt nod and took a slow breath, because slow breaths always calmed adults down. "Very well, then. Jared, what makes you think I would do anything to hurt you?'

"I didn't say you were trying to hurt me. You're just trying to trick me."

"Trick you?" Mary asked. "How?"

"I believe I understand," Chris said. He wiggled his fingers again and shifted into the Santa look he had worn a few moments before. Tracy looked around for cameras or strings. When she didn't see any, she realized she hadn't uncovered a single secret since she stepped through the mirror. Santa Command hadn't been very good at hiding their technology. Why was Chris' house so different?

Mary took one look at Santa Chris, and her face softened instantly. The harsh lines around her mouth were replaced with a glowing smile. Her eyes carried a spark that seemed to leap across the table and land in the corner of Chris' eyes.

Tracy looked at the two of them, and she could see how Mary fit in perfectly with Chris' Santa image. They both had gentle eyes and dimpled smiles.

"It's been a hundred years since I've seen you in that. I didn't think you still..." Mary's thoughts drifted off as she reached a finger up to dab at her eye.

"A hundred years? Come on!" Jared's snotty voice broke through the moment, and they all turned to look at him.

Tracy gave him a nasty look. Even she knew better than to be that rude.

"What?" he said. "Are you going to tell me you believe all of this stuff? They're playing with our minds."

"I..." Tracy began. "Well, I..."

Chris and Mary watched her as she struggled to find the truth. There was a war happening inside her, between all of the proof she had collected over the course of the night and the gnawing feeling in her gut that had begun sometime in Chris' presence. She spoke timidly as she pulled at the cuffs of her coat. "Well, there is that dust that makes people see things."

"Right," Jared said smugly. "And the zombie Santas, and that ride he has in the barn."

Chris gave a weary sigh. His Santa image slipped

off of him, but he didn't quite return to his normal self. His skin turned pasty and paper thin as if his previous appearance had been a costume as much as the Santa outfit was. Even his clothes seemed looser on him. The whole effect made him seem much, much older. "Well, I can't argue with the first two. Unfortunately, the world has changed over the centuries, and many things have become a necessity. I can assure you, however, that the sleigh ride I took you on, was one hundred percent genuine."

Jared leaned back in his chair and folded his arms across his chest. "Yeah, whatever."

"What about jets?" Tracy suggested. "There could have been jets on the sleigh. That would have made the ride real."

"Did you forget that we just popped back into the barn? How do you explain that, Miss I Wanna Be A Scientist?"

Tracy had no explanation. She'd forgotten about that part.

Chris saved her from having to answer. "Well, I suppose I could have a theme park ride in my barn. Or I could have dusted you like the Inklings do. I could have done any number of things to trick you." He paused long enough to make his next his next words seem very important. "But I haven't."

"I don't believe you," Jared said flatly.

Chris folded his hands on the table in front of him. He thumbs circled around each other as if he were weaving together his answer. Once again, Tracy felt like something important was about to be said. "Let me ask you both something. What makes you so sure there isn't magic in this world?"

Tracy answered first. "Everything has a scientific explanation." It was what she had believed her entire life, and every moment she'd spent in school had confirmed that. Sure, she'd seen magicians at parties, but she'd also seen books in the public library that showed just how they did all of those tricks. Fairies didn't exist, unicorns weren't hiding somewhere deep in the forest, and even Santa himself, was a corporation with a bunch of gadgets that made people think Santa was magical.

"I see. And do you have an explanation for everything you've seen tonight?"

Tracy squirmed a little in her seat. "Sort of."

"Sort of?" Chris asked.

"Well, not all of it. That was my plan, to figure out how everything worked. I had a hypothesis." And when your hypothesis is proven incorrect, you need to modify it. Beth had said that earlier. Tracy had proven her hypothesis in so many ways by finding the loading zone and spotting the jets on the sleigh and seeing the computer files. But there were other things she wasn't sure she could explain—her cast, the portal, the ride on Chris' sleigh. Even though she could create an explanation, they had all felt different, like they couldn't be real, but they were. Those things all suggested magic. Could her hypothesis be wrong? She shook her head. Her beliefs were cemented firmly into her brain. "There's no way one person could visit all of those houses in one night. Not even you."

"He did once." Mary's voice was so soft and wistful that both Jared and Tracy looked at her. "When the world was young, and there weren't so many people."

Jared shook his head and muttered something under his breath.

"What was that?" Chris asked. "My hearing isn't as good as it once was." Although Tracy got the feeling he had heard perfectly.

Jared pushed himself to his feet. His fingers splayed across the kitchen table as he leaned on it. His face turned very red. "I said that if Santa and all of this magic were real, then I never would have lost my parents!" He kicked the chair behind him into the wall and stormed toward the door. Before he left, he looked at them one last time. He pointed his finger at each of them as if they were the ones responsible for his parents. "I'm going home, and if any of you try to stop me, I'm calling the police."

The second the door slammed shut, Chris stood

up. As he did so, the fragile elderly man from moments before shifted into the Chris that Tracy had first met. He tugged on the hem of his vest and squared his shoulders. "Are you ready?"

"What are we gonna do?" Tracy asked him.

"We're going to see some magic."

CHAPTER THIRTY

Jared

Jared stormed out of the kitchen door and straight into the middle of a forest. The snow was deeper there, wrapping around his feet and snaking up his ankles. He tried not to mind it, but his socks were getting wet. He thought for a second about going back, but there were crazy people in the kitchen. At least with the snow, he knew exactly what to expect. He didn't know where he was going, and he certainly didn't know how to get there, but his feet were moving, and for now, that was enough.

After a few minutes, he found a small river. It was frozen over. He didn't stop to think that he hadn't seen any frozen creeks yet in Alabama this year, although he was certain he was still in his home state. Even if he had thought about the creeks, he would have rationalized it by saying the hot chocolate was still showing him things that weren't really there. He'd also been given hot chocolate the night of his worst nightmare ever. They'd forced the images into him, and the words from the dream still echoed in his head in the inky black of the night.

The workers at Santa Command had been very good at playing with his mind. When he first came to live with Beth, she brought him there, hoping that the "magic" would convince him that things were going to be okay. They showed him flying reindeer, the Inklings (deformed squirrels in his opinion), and Santas traveling up and down chimneys in a puff of smoke. They'd even sent him to Chris' house and insisted he'd been to the North Pole.

As a child, yes, he would have called it magic. As an eleven-year-old, an age he liked to think of as young adult, he knew that all of those things were tricks designed to keep the public in the dark. There was no magic. Santa existed, but only as a club of old men playing dress up.

Chris may have been retired, but he was still one of them. He was still part of the joke that had been played on the world for centuries. Jared didn't wish to be any part of that joke. Any time Beth talked about work, Jared would mutter something about homework, retreat to his room, and lay on his bed with his iPod blasting into his ears. The sound took him into his head where he could leave the world behind him. Chris spoke about magic, but the only real magic Jared could imagine was the kind that would make him forget. For him, music was magic.

As Jared followed the river, he shuffled through his mental playlist until he came up with something angry, something Beth would forbid him to listen to because of the four-letter words in the lyrics. He found the perfect song and screamed it at the top of his lungs.

He stomped through the snow for a long time, bringing each foot up and pounding it back to the ground. It made him feel better, like he was accomplishing something. Or maybe it just made him feel not so lost. Because that was how he'd felt for one year and forty-five days. No. It was past midnight. Forty-six days.

He stomped and screamed. The ground quivered beneath him. He smiled.

Stomp. Scream. *Stomp*. Scream. *Stomp*.

Crack!

Without realizing it, he'd stomped onto the ice. It was a very thin patch of ice, with very cold water running beneath it. And as he plunged into the water, he forgot to scream.

CHAPTER THIRTY-ONE

Tracy

Chris whispered some instructions to his wife, then said, "Follow me," to Tracy. He led her into a hallway where he poked around in a closet. Well, closet wasn't the right word. It was more like "Place where he stored every object ever created."

The sight of Chris rummaging around in that closet with his rear end sticking out of the mess was enough to make Tracy laugh.

Chris tossed his belongings into the hallway as he searched. There were coats, of course, and a vacuum cleaner, some boxes of Kleenex, a few board games, a Jello mold, a hamster cage, a painting of a seal on the beach, a ball of string, a vase, a kite. The list went on and on. Tracy even thought she saw a dog peek out of there at one point.

Finally, Chris emerged with a small canvas bag held

high in the air. He handed it to Tracy. When she opened it, she found a pair of socks covered in red and green reindeer and a pair of fur lined boots. They were just Tracy's size. But even crazier, the socks looked just like a pair both she and Pim had gotten for Christmas one year. From Santa. Her chest tightened as she traced the outline of a reindeer with her finger. Her eyes blurred over.

"You'll want to change out of those wet sneakers," he said.

"Oh, right." She snapped out of her daze and squished her toes up inside her shoes. She hadn't realized until then that her toes felt numb. Her own shoes and socks were still soaked from walking through the snow.

"Thank you," she said, although what she really wanted to ask was, "How did you know?"

Once she had changed, and they were on their way back to the barn, Chris said to her, "You still have questions."

Tracy shrugged, a gesture that made her feel very small inside that big coat. Chris knew so much. She could chalk it up to the hot chocolate like Jared had, but she didn't want to. She had sneaked out on Christmas Eve to find the truth. What if the truth really couldn't be explained with a science project? She stuffed her hands in her pockets, because she couldn't find the right thing to say. Too much was whirling about in her mind.

"Okay," Chris said softly, "how about we start with this? You didn't leave with Jared."

"No." Tracy had seen no sense in that. All he was doing was throwing a hissy fit. It must have been terrible to lose his parents, but running away wasn't going to fix anything. "But that doesn't mean I don't agree with some of the things he said."

"Such as?"

She took a deep breath. The cold air filled her lungs and gave her courage. Although, she wasn't sure why she needed the courage to speak her beliefs. Maybe it was because her beliefs didn't seem that solid anymore. "Magic can't be real."

"And why not?"

She looked up at him thoughtfully. Their gazes locked as the two of them trudged along in the snow. The moonlight reflected in his eyes, and for a moment, he seemed not quite human. People were hard edges and solid facts. He was more like a teddy bear come to life. She wanted to believe him. No, that wasn't exactly right. She wanted to believe *in* him. "Earlier tonight, you said you were Santa."

"I did."

"What does that mean, exactly?"

Chris took in a long, slow breath, then blew it out.

His breath turned into little snowflakes dancing inside a cloud, then fell softly onto his belly and melted. "How about I tell you a story?"

"I think that will be okay." All stories had some truth in them, and sometimes they were easier to tell than the facts.

"Once upon a time, a man and his wife lived in a very small, very poor village, far across the ocean. They had no children, but that was okay, because their village was full of children who spent their days laughing and playing in the streets. The couple enjoyed the sound of laughter so much, that whenever a child was in need, they did what they could to help. Sometimes, it was milk for a crying baby. Sometimes, it was new clothing for a child who only had tattered rags."

"That was nice of them," Tracy said.

"They did what they could, and because the children were happy, they were happy. Soon, the couple became known throughout the village, but the villagers were often too embarrassed to ask for help. The old man and his wife were smart, though." Chris tapped his finger to his temple. "They got word out to the children and told them to slide a letter under the couple's front door if they needed anything. If the children left their shoes outside their house at night, the old man would sneak little gifts or coins into them. Does that remind you of anything?"

Tracy knew where this was going. "Is that where Santa Command got the idea for everything? Children's letters and stockings by the fireplace."

He touched his finger to her nose. "You're very smart, but I'm sure you also know many things changed over the years."

"Like adding the reindeer and only giving gifts on Christmas?"

"And the red suit." He tugged at the collar of her coat, and she giggled. At the sound of her laughter, his smile spread wide across his face. "So anyway, these traditions continued for decades, until the man and the woman were very old. They were so old in fact, that the man could no longer leave his bed, not even to stand by the street and listen to the children's laughter. This made him very sad."

"Did he die?" Tracy asked, even though she was afraid of the answer. She didn't want the old man to have died alone in his bed.

They reached the barn doors, and Chris turned to her. He tilted his head and narrowed his eyes as if he were studying her. "This is the part where the story becomes fantastical. And I must ask that you believe every word."

Tracy eyed him carefully, ready to say that she couldn't promise anything. As her mouth formed the answer, his body seemed to fuzz around the edges, and for a split second, she saw him as a younger man. He wore a cloak that looked like it came from a picture in her history book. Then, he turned back into Chris, the guy who looked like a well-dressed grandfather. She could have chalked it up to the late hour and the fact that she was so tired, but she didn't. "What is it?" she asked in a whisper.

He held up a finger, telling her to wait just a moment as he opened the barn doors and led her to a dark corner near the front. There, he knelt beside a small wooden chest and placed his hand on top, as if he wasn't ready to open it just yet.

Tracy sat down beside him. He hadn't said a word since entering the barn, and so she hadn't either. Her heart fluttered, and she was surprised at how much she needed to hear his story. She stared at him, wide-eyed.

Chris continued. "One night, just as the old man thought he would draw his last breath, a creature appeared before him. Some might call her an angel. Some would say fairy. All he knew was that she was about to change his life." He paused, drawing out the moment until Tracy sucked in her breath. "She granted his desire to do good in the world, by granting him two gifts—magic and immortality."

Tracy sat up straight. No one was immortal. It wasn't possible.

Chris must have noticed the doubt in her eyes, because he said, "Please, wait until you've heard and seen everything." And with that, he opened the box.

CHAPTER THIRTY-TWO

Tracy

A brilliant, golden light filled the barn, blinding Tracy for a moment until she blinked a few times and got used to it. It came from the box. If Tracy had been asked to draw the light, she would have drawn a sunshine with glittering rays shooting out of it in every direction.

"Whoa!" She scooted backward, afraid all of that light would burn her, even though it didn't feel hot, just tingly.

"This is the source of my magic," Chris said, but he said it slowly, like he was testing the impact of each word on her. "I've carried it through the centuries and across the ocean. As long as I have this, the world has a Santa Claus."

"But how..." Tracy couldn't finish. She knew it couldn't be real, but it was. It was the color of her cast, the color of the portal, the color of every magical thing she had seen that night. Her skin prickled with the same tingles she had felt time and again whenever she encountered something magical.

Excitement threatened to burst from her veins as her new hypothesis formed.

Magic. Was. Real.

And she was looking right at it.

"How does it work?" she asked.

"Watch this." He scooped his hand into the box and brought up a ball of light, barely larger than his palm. He blew gently across the surface. The golden colors swirled and settled into a picture of Tracy standing by Pim's bedside only a few days ago. Pim's dark hair was spread across her pillow. She was too pale, and she stared off at nothing. That vacant gaze sucked away all of Tracy's excitement. Her stomach turned.

"I'm going to fix you. I know what to do," said the Tracy inside the ball. A TV flickered in the background.

Pim lay in her bed, staring, blinking. Her fingers tapped up and down on the covers. Tracy never knew if Pim did that on purpose or if it was just her nerves moving them.

Tracy went on, speaking very low as if she was afraid someone would come in and hear what she was saying. "I heard your mom talking to my mom on the phone. There's a doctor, and he can fix you. No one has the money, but I know how to get it. I promise you, everything's gonna be okay."

Just then a commercial came on the TV, reminding children to send in their lists to Santa Command. It caught Pim's attention. She looked at the TV and gasped. Then, one word came from her mouth, "Saaaanta."

"Yes!" Tracy said. "Yes! That's how I'm going to help you. I'm going to find Santa." She hadn't told Pim her whole plan, because there was no need. The point was, Tracy was going to fix her cousin, and her cousin understood!

The image disappeared from the ball. Tracy had tears in her eyes. "I let her down," she said while rubbing her sleeve across her cheek. "I messed everything up."

Chris considered that for a moment, then with a regretful tone in his voice, he said, "Tracy, I have something else to show you."

Tracy nodded. She was upset that she hadn't been able to help Pim, but she was ashamed of what she had done that night. It was time to own up to it. "Is this about the computer?"

His answer was to blow another breath across the ball of light. The scene shifted to a forest, one with a dry, barren ground and skinny, skeleton trees. In the middle of the forest was a wall. That wall didn't have bricks or cinder blocks or any of the normal things that make up walls. It was a shimmery, flowing barrier that looked like the surface of a soap bubble. It reached all the way up to the sky.

"What's that?" Tracy asked.

"A mistake." He looked at her, and she knew that he meant it was her mistake.

"Can it be fixed?" She didn't know what it was, but at that moment, she would have given anything to fix it. Not only did the bubble look scary, it looked wrong in a way that made Tracy's head spin.

"I don't know," Chris said honestly. "In order to fix the computer, they had to stop time, but when they started it again, this is what happened. They're lost, Tracy, in another time. And I don't know how to get them back."

"Lost? Is it just Santa Command?"

Chris shook his head. The forest in the ball zoomed out to show a map of the United States.

Tracy saw little pinpricks of light, indicating big cites, but in Florida, Georgia, and Alabama, she saw nothing. All three were blacked out.

Chris pointed to the dark section. "The entire Southeastern sector."

Tracy gasped. She thought she'd just crashed a few programs and that Santa Command could run things manually if they had to. Why hadn't she thought about the consequences? "My...My parents are gone." Did that mean she wouldn't see her parents or Pim ever again? "Why didn't you tell me this before?"

"I was hoping I'd come up with an idea." He let the ball slip back into the box. "But I'm old, and the world just doesn't work like it used to."

"What do you mean it doesn't work? Time can't be altered. No matter what the world is like, time is constant. Just like science."

Except, if there was magic, then maybe the world wasn't as constant as she'd always thought. And the more she thought about it, she remembered another scientist who knew that too.

"Einstein," Tracy said. She'd done a book report about him in fifth grade, and that book report was forming into an idea.

"Yes?" Chris narrowed his eyes like he was trying to see the cogs and gears turning in her brain.

Tracy didn't remember exactly what the book had said, but she had the general idea. "He said that it was possible to travel through time if we had the right catalyst, something to set it off."

"What would set it off?" Chris took her hand, encouraging her to figure it out.

"Something big, like a star exploding." And then she knew. She had a plan that would bring her family and everyone else in her sector, back to the right time.

While the plan took shape, she chewed on her knuckle. They needed a plastic bag and a cloth bag and maybe two handfuls of the magic sitting before them. It was the perfect combination of science and magic. "I know what to do," she said, hoping she had calculated correctly. If she overestimated, she could blow up half of Alabama. "We're gonna need the sleigh."

Chris smiled, like he never doubted she would come up with a solution. With a tilt of his head, he indicated the other side of the barn. "Do you see what's back there?"

Tracy turned. Behind her, the horse stalls transformed. Yellow sparkles twirled around the broken wood and splintered signs until everything looked brand new. There were eight stalls, freshly painted and with name signs on each one. The one that said "ond" earlier now said, "Donder," and poking his head above the stall door, was a magnificent reindeer.

Tracy jumped to her feet. "Are those...?"

"They certainly are," Chris said. "Are you ready to go for another ride?"

"One second." She pulled her neck pouch from beneath her shirt and emptied all of the contents onto the ground. Chris raised an eyebrow at some of the things she had collected. She chose not to comment and held the pouch over the magic box. Before she took any, she stopped herself. "Can I have some of this?"

"If that's part of your plan," Chris said. "But we better hurry. Time is waiting."

While Tracy filled the bag, Chris harnessed up the reindeer. When the bag was full, Tracy plucked an empty Ziploc bag from her pile on the ground and ran to the sleigh. Within moments, they were soaring over the forest once again.

As they flew, she explained her plan and how she knew it was going to work. After all, she had performed an accidental test of the experiment back in the warehouse. When she had finished, Chris punched a red button on the dashboard. It was small and tucked in a corner, so Tracy hadn't noticed it. A TV screen appeared in the middle of the dash, where before there had been nothing but a red, wooden board. His sleigh wasn't old-fashioned after all.

Mary's face popped onto the screen, and Chris gave her a few directions. Based on the urgent way he spoke to his wife, Tracy knew her plan was going to work.

She bounced up and down in the seat, chanting "Faster! Faster!" under her breath, hoping that would somehow make the reindeer pick up their speed.

They were nearly at the edge of the forest when a cry far below them cut through her thoughts.

"Help!"

CHAPTER THIRTY-THREE

Jared

Jared was submerged up to his armpits. After he'd fallen into the river, he'd kicked hard and fast, but his hands slipped right across the ice, and he couldn't pull himself out. The only thing that had kept him from slipping under completely was his grip on a tree branch frozen into the ice.

He didn't know how long he'd been there. It was probably minutes, but it felt like hours. He was so cold. He couldn't feel his legs anymore. His hands were throbbing, and he didn't think he could hold on to the branch much longer.

That was the moment he looked up and saw the sleigh and reindeer flying above him. He didn't know whether they were real or imaginary visions, and he didn't care.

"Help!" he called, but his throat was frozen, and

the word was barely a whisper. They couldn't hear him. Soon, they would be too far away. A knot formed inside his chest. This could be his only chance. He cleared his throat, then called out louder. "Help!"

A small face appeared over the edge of the sleigh. *Tracy!*

"There!" She pointed down at him. "It's Jared!"

As the reindeer guided the sleigh downward, Jared cried with relief. They came for him. Chris came.

They landed. Tracy immediately popped out of the sleigh and ran for him.

"Hang on," Chris called to her as he pulled a thick, coiled rope out of the sleigh. He tied one end to a bar on the back of the sleigh and handed the rest to Tracy. "Toss this to him, but don't get too close. We don't want you falling in too."

"Got it." She did just as she was told and tossed the rope to Jared when she was about five feet away. It smacked him hard in the face, but he was too relieved to snap at her. He didn't have the voice anyway.

He let go of the log and threw his arms as quickly as he could around the rope. When he did, the coil unraveled, and he slipped under the water.

"No!" he cried, but all that came out of his mouth were bubbles. He kicked furiously as he slid further under. He clamped his mouth shut and pulled on the rope. The rope uncoiled, foot after foot of it slipping through the hole in the ice, like it wasn't attached to anything at all. What good was the rope if it was too long to help him? His lungs burned. Every part of his body hurt. He shut his eyes. *Please let me get out of here. Please. Please let me get out of here.*

Suddenly, the rope tightened. He didn't realize he was clutching it to his chest. He held on as his body inched up through the water until finally, he burst through the surface.

He gasped and spit. "Get me! Help!"

Chris guided the reindeer forward as they pulled the sleigh, and the sleigh pulled the rope, and the rope pulled Jared. He held tightly to that rope with one hand and dug his fingers into the ice with the other, scooting himself forward until he was finally out of the river.

As soon as she could, Tracy grabbed his arm and helped him to his feet. Her eyes were as big as lumps of coal, and he could tell she was scared. But nothing could compare to how scared he'd been.

He only stood for a second before he crumpled to his knees. His legs were too frozen to support him.

Chris raced to his side with a large, brown bundle in his arms. It was a blanket, which he wrapped around Jared. The old man was dressed in his Santa outfit again, and he knelt beside Jared on the ground.

Jared let Chris take his hands. Warmth filled the

boy instantly, like he was being dipped in a hot bath. It wasn't coming from the blanket, but from Chris. It entered through his palms, snaked up his arms, and filled his body. It wasn't possible, but it was happening, and he was grateful. Within seconds, his clothes were dry, and his bones stopped shivering.

Jared took a few breaths before he said what he had to. "Thank you."

"You are quite welcome." Chris let go of Jared and pushed himself to his feet.

"Wait," Tracy said, like something had just clicked in her mind. "We flew over the forest when you had the ability to simply pop us straight to Alabama. You knew Jared had fallen through the ice."

"You did?" Jared felt his face heating up just like it had in the kitchen. "Why didn't you come sooner?"

"My dear boy, when will you learn to believe in me? I'll always come for you."

"But how did you know where he was?" asked Tracy.

"Haven't you heard the song? I know when you're sleeping. I know when you're awake." Chris tapped the side of his head. "I've got my own personal GPS right here. I knew we'd get there in time."

"But I didn't," Jared wailed. "I thought I was...I was going to..."

With his face all scrunched up and tears pooling at the corners of his eyes, Jared didn't feel like the angry kid from before. It had been terrifying, sliding down into that water, not knowing if he was ever going to breathe again. Chris may have known what he was doing, but no one told him.

"Jared," Tracy said quietly. "I'm glad you're okay."

Jared swiped his sleeve under his nose and looked at Tracy, like he was seeing her for the first time ever. "Thank you."

Tracy squirmed a little, tugging at the hem of her Santa coat. "You're welcome."

Chris cleared his throat, and Jared was glad for the interruption. His face switched from concerned caregiver to man with a mission. "Jared, since you're feeling better, how about I give you a job?" He didn't wait for Jared to answer. He simply turned on his heel and walked toward the sleigh.

Jared stood still for moment, wondering why Chris was in such a hurry.

As the old man hefted himself into the sleigh, Tracy tugged on his sleeve. "Come on!"

The two of them took their places on either side of Chris, and before Jared could ask any questions, the wintery forest had vanished. Chris, Jared, and Tracy, along with the sleigh and all eight reindeer were now sitting on the edge of a forest. On one side of them were bare winter trees, but on the other side was a gigantic, pulsing wall.

CHAPTER THIRTY-FOUR

Santa Command—Phil's office
December 25th
0410 hours

Walt ushered Phil into the office, then slammed the door shut behind them. Phil's framed "Employee of the Year" certificates bounced against the walls.

Phil backed up against his desk. He gripped the edge to hold himself steady.

Walt stood before him, his face glowing Santa suit red. His stubby finger sliced the air between them. "First, you bring the girl here against my orders. Then, you let her get loose. And then…" Walt's face turned a deep shade of purple as he geared up to explode. "And then, you purposely give her access to our computer. She crashes it, and of course you decide to fix it by knocking thirty four million people out of time. And after all that, I still don't think you understand the magnitude of what you've done. If you did, you would have handed in your badge two hours ago."

Walt paused. His breaths came in short, angry puffs as he stared at Phil's collar.

No, he stared at the ID badge dangling from Phil's collar.

Phil unclipped the badge, which had been a source of pride for him for so long, and with shaky fingers, handed it to his boss. "You know why I brought her here."

Walt stuffed the badge in his pocket. "And you know why you shouldn't have. I want you out of Santa Command by morning." He ripped one of Phil's certificates from the wall and threw it to the ground, then stomped out the door.

Shattered glass covered the floor like ice. It was almost pretty except Phil knew that it was a symbol of his failed career.

Phil shrugged sadly. Once the Inklings dusted him, he wouldn't remember the plaques or his job or anything real about the last fifteen years. He'd never spend another Christmas Eve squaring off against the kids, because this year, he'd lost.

Soon people would start waking up. A couple hundred of them would be wondering why Santa hadn't delivered their presents. The rest would be wondering why they couldn't call family in other states. Confusion would soon turn into panic, because for them, the rest of the world would simply disappear like someone took scissors and cut them away. Why hadn't he considered the consequences before he acted? Would *someone* eventually fix it?

Phil wondered if the night could have played out differently. What if he had wiped Tracy when he was supposed to? What if he had put a guard by her window at Santa Command so she couldn't escape? As Phil struggled to think of how he could have fixed the computer without stopping time, a message in red letters appeared across the bottom of his monitor.

Incoming Call. Press enter to accept.

What?

He pressed enter, and Mary's image popped up on the screen. "Good morning. It's been quite a night, hasn't it?"

Phil angled his screen, because he didn't think he was seeing it correctly. "How is this even possible? We're out of sync with you guys."

Mary smiled like she knew a secret. She'd always been good at keeping them. "You're probably wondering how I'm speaking to you. This is a recording which I uploaded to your main frame, programmed to run on every computer at this exact time."

Phil sighed miserably. Of course, she and Chris had found a way to scold him. At least, he wouldn't remember it for long. He looked forward to the Inkling dust.

"I know you think I'm probably going to yell," continued Mary, "but I'm not. This is far more important, and you need to listen to every word."

Phil sat up. Had they found a solution? He grabbed a pen and notepad.

"The first thing I'm going to give you is a warning, and the second is a request."

CHAPTER THIRTY-FIVE

Tracy

Tracy and Jared jumped out of the sleigh, Tracy with her pouch and Jared with the Ziploc bag so the magic was as far away from the plastic as possible. There was no way she would risk an explosion before they were ready.

The wall was even scarier in person. It stretched up as far as she could see, and it hummed, like there was an electrical current flowing through it. Jared reached out to touch it. Tracy grabbed his arm.

"You might not want to do that."

Why not?" he asked.

"Just a feeling. Here," she held out her neck pouch, "open your bag."

He held the gallon bag while Tracy poured the yellow magic into it. The first sparks zoomed around the bottom of the bag, like they were inside a washing machine. They were pretty angry about where they were being placed. Tracy quickly dumped the rest in, not caring that a couple of specs dropped to the ground. She had a feeling this wouldn't take long.

"Now, zip it up."

His fingers fumbled, and he nearly dropped the bag. "Ow! This stuff is getting hot."

"Oh, give it to me." Tracy zipped it up, even though the heat scorched her fingertips. Then, she threw it, hard and fast at the time wall.

The plastic bag stuck to the wall, sparking and hissing like a sparkler on the Fourth of July. Streaks of lightning scattered along the wall's surface away from the bag. That was why she didn't want Jared touching it. If it sizzled a plastic bag, she didn't want to see what it did to a boy.

The bag pulsed as the magic inside it heated up and expanded. The seams of the bag grew tight. The contents inside turned red with fury.

Tracy shouted, "Run!"

Tracy, Jared, and Chris dove for cover behind the sleigh. For extra protection, Chris wiggled his fingers and put up his own wall of magic on the other side of the sleigh, shielding them and the reindeer.

And then the magic exploded.

Jared plugged his ears and closed his eyes, Chris rested on the ground with his back against the sleigh, but Tracy crouched behind the sleigh and watched it all.

Balls of fire rocketed from the bag and punched through the time wall, shattering it into a billion pieces. On the other side, time seemed frozen, but then it popped into fast forward. The fireballs rushed through the forest, ripping it to shreds. Baseball sized rocks hammered their shield. Branches and dry leaves blasted against it. For several long minutes, the shield quivered, but it held.

When it was finally over, Tracy stood up and gasped. The wall was definitely gone, but so was at least three acres of forest. In its place, sat a black, smoking pit.

Jared stood beside her and let out a low whistle.

"Um, maybe I used a little too much magic," Tracy said.

"You think?"

Chris stood up too, wobbling as he did so.

"Are you okay?" Tracy tucked her hand under his elbow and helped him right himself.

"Thank you, my dear." Chris removed a white handkerchief from his coat pocket and dabbed his forehead. "That was quite exciting, wasn't it?"

"Sorry," she said while she made a mental note to write down the amount of magic she had used and the results. Good scientists always kept records.

"Hey, did you ever think that maybe magic is just an undiscovered element? I bet they'd even let you name it. You could call it Santanium."

Chris let out a belly laugh. "I wouldn't classify it as undiscovered. Those who believe have always known about it."

"I guess," she said, but she tucked the idea into the back of her mind for future hypotheses. "So, what now?"

Chris climbed into the sleigh and punched the red button on the dashboard. Phil's face appeared on the screen this time.

"Are we back?" Phil asked.

"It seems like it," Chris said. "Now, I believe Mary asked you for a list."

Phil smiled with relief. "147 houses. I'm uploading the coordinates to your sleigh now."

Chris clapped his hands together and called down to Tracy and Jared. "Come on you two. It's not every Christmas I come out of retirement. Aren't you going to join me?"

Tracy was ready to go. There was still lots to do and very little time left in the night.

The two kids scrambled into the sleigh. After Chris wiggled his fingers, they were all sitting in a swamp with Spanish moss hanging from the trees. And it was hot.

The Cyprus Grove looked familiar to Tracy, like somewhere she'd once visited on a school field trip. "Are we...?"

"Precisely," Chris answered. "The Green Swamp. Fifteen miles from your neighborhood."

She scanned the area and found what she was looking for—a boardwalk winding through the trees and over a section of the swamp. She *had* been there on a field trip. Her teacher had led them across the boardwalk, searching for signs of wildlife. All they found were spider webs and bird poop. She felt like the whole trip had been a waste of time, much like this second visit to the swamp. They had 147 houses to take care of. "The sun's gonna be up soon. If you can pop from place to place, why didn't you just take us to the first house?"

"Because we needed to prepare first."

"Prepare?"

"I can't deliver presents without my assistants, can I?" Chris rubbed his hands together, then placed one on each of her shoulders. A river of yellow air flowed from his hands and down her coat. Her shoulders tingled a little, but other than that, she felt nothing as the oversized Santa coat shrunk into a red and white fitted jacket that Tracy could have worn to a fancy party. It wasn't too hot anymore, and Tracy looked like she fit in perfectly with the theming of Chris' ancient sleigh.

Jared sat wide-eyed on the other side of Chris. "Are you gonna do that," he gulped, "to me?" After everything he'd just seen, he was still struggling with his belief in magic.

Tracy held out her arm.

"It's real," she said. "All of this is."

Jared rubbed her white fur cuff between his fingers. He pinched his eyes shut and said to Chris, "Go ahead."

Chris once again rubbed his hands together, then placed them on Jared's shoulders. That same yellow river of magic flowed across Jared's chest. One corner of his mouth tilted up in a smile as he saw his new outfit. He'd gone from a kid in a brown striped sweater to a kid in a red striped sweater. It was enough to make him look like he belonged with Santa, but not enough to make him stand out in a crowd of other eleven year olds.

"Thanks," Jared said. "Again."

"Anytime," Chris said with a wink. "Now, as Tracy said, the sun is almost up. We have a job to do."

"Are we going to pop over to the houses now?" Tracy asked. She hadn't admitted it to anyone, but traveling by magic was starting to thrill her. It was like having her very own Star Trek transporter.

"My dear girl, haven't you ever heard of making an entrance?" Chris snapped the reins, and the reindeer leaped into the sky.

CHAPTER THIRTY-SIX

Santa Command—Loading Bay
December 25th
0430 hours

All of the remaining presents had been loaded into bags and placed on the platform. Phil stepped back and examined the pile skeptically. It was an awful lot of presents to deliver in an hour, and there was no way it would fit in one sleigh. At least, it wouldn't fit in one of their current sleighs. He'd never seen Chris' sleigh in person. In all of the pictures, it looked like a rickety little thing that would blow apart in a good stiff wind. But who was he to question magic? All he knew was that Mary believed this would work.

Phil signaled to an Inkling who climbed to the top of the pile. Once there, the little creature grabbed a fistful of dust from one of her pouches and threw it up over her head. The Inkling and the pile were gone before the dust settled.

CHAPTER THIRTY-SEVEN

Tracy

A single red bag appeared in the back of the sleigh. Tracy reached back to touch it. It was the same slippery, silky material as before, but this time it felt tingly too. Did it have magic that the other bags didn't? She poked at a few places on the fabric. It acted like a mini trampoline, springing back into shape after each poke. When she poked something soft and squishy, she heard a squeal.

Tracy yanked her hand back.

A small guinea pig-sized lump made its way under the surface of the bag and up to the top. An elf face popped out of the opening. "Watch what you're doing. I don't remember poking you."

The elf had a sprout like ponytail on the top of her head, just like the one Tracy had seen earlier that night. "No, but I remember you from the rooftop." She also remembered the wolves and the troll and scowled.

"Well, you shouldn't have run from me," the elf said simply. "I do love a chase."

Jared had been watching the whole thing and started laughing. "Even I know better than to mess with one of the Inklings."

Tracy might have turned her back on the little creature just out of spite, but when she wasn't snarling or sitting on top of her, she looked kind of cute. "Inkling?" Tracy tested the sound of the word. It seemed to apply to the girl staring back at her.

"Yeah." She climbed out of the bag and perched on top. The wind from the moving sleigh made her do a backwards somersault. She balled her tiny fists up in the material, holding on tight so she didn't get blown away. "Inklings. Santa's helpers. You know, we're what people call *elves*." When she said "elves," she made a face like she was tasting sour milk.

"You're not elves?" Tracy asked.

"Here we go again." Jared rolled his eyes. "Can we skip the speech, Sasha?"

"Us? Elves?" Sasha turned her head to the right and spit. "Ptooey! Those foul little rats don't have one ounce of magic in their bodies."

Jared turned around and sunk back into his seat. It was obvious he had heard this a million times, but Tracy hadn't, and she was very interested.

"And you have magic?" Tracy asked. Of course

they did. She'd seen them transform into wolves and a giant troll only a few hours earlier. She just hadn't believed it was magic at the time.

The Inkling smiled smugly at Tracy. "We're *made* of magic. Watch this." She closed her eyes. Her body melted into a ball of yellow swirls, exactly like the magic that had filled the box back in Chris' barn.

"That's amazing!" Tracy said.

Chris kept his eyes on his reindeer as they soared over the Cyprus trees. He smiled as if he knew that Sasha was showing off. "The time came when I needed someone to help me with deliveries. I made a simple wish, opened the box, and they came running out." Chris spoke fondly of the memory. "I haven't been able to tame them since."

The Inkling blew a raspberry at Chris, but she did it with a smile. Sasha's round brown eyes said everything. She adored that man, her Santa Claus.

Tracy realized it was the first time she had ever thought of Chris as Santa, and she wondered how she hadn't known it the moment she met him. Now, as she looked at his profile—his long, white beard, his rosy cheeks, his shining eyes—she knew there was no way he could ever be anything but Santa. So why did he quit? "Hey, Chris? Why did you...?"

"First house!" Sasha squeaked over Chris' shoulder. "Let's do this!"

CHAPTER THIRTY-EIGHT

Tracy

They landed on a roof two streets over from Tracy's house. As soon as the sleigh stopped moving, Sasha dove back into the bag and came up with a pile of presents ten times larger than her tiny body. She balanced them easily in a pile above her head. Chris took a few. The kids grabbed the rest so Sasha could hop out and run over to the chimney.

"This way," Chris nudged Tracy out of the sleigh, then marched over to the chimney without looking back to see if Tracy and Jared were following. They always did.

Chris jumped first. As his feet left the rooftop, he and his stack of presents dissolved into a mist that floated down the chimney.

Jared took a step backward. "Um, I can't do that." And he looked like he didn't want to either.

Tracy looked at Sasha, unsure of whether to

follow Chris or side with Jared. "How does this work? We're..." she searched for the right word, "...human." Believing in magic was one thing. *Becoming* it was something else entirely.

"But I'm not." Sasha stuffed a fist into a small bag hanging from her belt and pulled out a handful of dust. "The clock's ticking. Are you gonna trust me or not?"

Tracy sighed. She'd already accepted magic was real. This was just one more experiment that would prove her theory. "Fine." She took a deep breath and jumped.

Sasha tossed a handful of dust into the air over the chimney. As Tracy passed through it, her entire body, from her scalp to her toes, shivered with magic. It was the best thrill ride ever. Going down the chimney was like going down a water slide, except she was the water. She popped out at the bottom and landed on her feet, solid once more. "Wow. That was—"

Chris grabbed her arm and pulled her out of the way, just as Jared came shooting out after her. He wasn't nearly as graceful, and his stack of presents tumbled to the ground. Jared grabbed hold of the mantle as he caught his breath. "Wow."

"I know," Tracy answered him.

Somewhere in the house, a floorboard creaked.

Chris put a finger to his lips, and the children froze.

They all looked at the staircase, where ten bare toes appeared on the top step.

CHAPTER THIRTY-NINE

Santa Command—Control Room 8
December 25th
0435 hours

The entire control room was silent as Phil watched the screen, his fingers tapping nervously on his knees. He'd been allowed back into the control room to watch, with Walt, naturally peering over his shoulder. They had protocol to follow whenever a child got out of bed while the Santas were in the house. But this wasn't just one of the Santas. This was Chris. And he was different.

All of their Santas were normal guys who had displayed extraordinary acts of kindness toward others. They were recruited because of their very nature—they wanted to make the world better. They agreed to being hypnotized, because they understood that their job did not need to be recognized or remembered. The deliveries just needed to happen, and they were willing to do it.

But because they were nice, normal guys following a program in their minds, they had no ability to improvise. If children got out of bed, Santa Command saw and corrected it, usually with Inkling magic. The Santas never knew about it and didn't have enough magic to do anything, even if they did know.

But now, here was Chris, making deliveries for the first time in over a century, and he was about to be caught by a child.

This was his operation. It had been from the very beginning. There was no protocol for him. So, all Phil could do was sit and watch.

CHAPTER FORTY

Jared

A girl, maybe six or seven years old, with short, blond pigtails and a yellow nightgown stepped off of the last stair and into the living room. She bounced on her toes, but didn't come any closer. There were an awful lot of people in her living room, and she was a tiny girl who was supposed to be in bed.

Jared knew exactly what Santa Command did in this situation. He kept his eye on Sasha, expecting the Inkling to yank some dust from her bag and toss it into the kid's face. But that didn't happen. Sasha stood perfectly still, watching Chris in much the same way the little girl was watching him.

Chris knelt down on one knee and waved the little girl toward him. "Hello, Sophie. Are you ready for Christmas?"

She ran over and jumped on his knee.

Chris wobbled a little, but kept his balance. "Whoa, there," he said. "I'm an old man you know."

Sophie reached one finger up to touch his beard. As soon as she touched it, he said, "Boo!" and she yanked her finger back and giggled.

"You're the real Santa, aren't you?" she asked. "You know, not the fake ones from the malls and stuff. I have to know. It's important."

Chris wrapped his arms around her, holding her steady on his knee. "Why do you ask?"

"Well, my dad..." She stopped and scrubbed her fingers under her eyes. Then she clammed up again.

Chris filled in the rest for her. "Your dad said he had something for you, didn't he? That only the real Santa could deliver it."

Sophie's eyes lit up. "Yes! He said it in a dream. He couldn't tell me in person, because he's not..." She looked from Jared to Tracy to Sasha, then leaned in to Chris as if she were telling him a secret that the others weren't supposed to hear. But Jared was standing right next to Chris, and he heard her whisper. "He's not here anymore."

Jared felt a knot form inside of his chest. There were pictures all over the living room of Sophie with her mom and dad. He wondered how and when she'd lost him, even though he didn't want either thought in his head. He knelt beside the tree and started arranging the presents they'd brought, just to get his mind on something else.

"Jared," Chris said, "hand her that blue one, will you?"

Jared picked up the flat, rectangular present and gave it to Sophie.

She carefully pulled back the shiny blue wrapper. Inside was an old picture book with part of the cover torn off so only half of a sand castle was visible. Sophie clapped her hand to her mouth like she was afraid her excitement would escape.

Jared didn't understand what was so special about an old book until Sophie opened the cover. There, on the first page, was a message scrawled in blue ink.

My dearest Sophie, I know how much you always loved this book, and I hope that every time you read it, you will think of me and remember the times I read it to you. All my love. Daddy

Sophie threw her arms around Chris' neck. "In the dream, he said the real Santa would give me the present. He said I already knew what it was." She wasn't whispering anymore, but even if she had spoken only to Chris, Jared would still have known what she said. He would have known, because just over one year ago, he'd had the same dream. He once thought it had been brought on by Mary's hot chocolate, but he was wrong.

Jared felt like his lungs didn't work anymore. He grabbed on to his knees and sucked in as much air as he could.

Tracy knelt down beside him. "Are you okay?"

Jared didn't know anymore. All he knew for sure was that Chris was the real Santa.

CHAPTER FORTY-ONE

Tracy

"What do you need?" Tracy asked Jared.

He was very pale, and his arms were shaking. "S… Santa."

"What about him?"

Jared kept his head down and breathed deeply. After another long moment where he didn't say anything, he jumped to his feet. He'd gone from a crumpled ball of mush to a jumble of excitement in less than a second. He paced back and forth in front of the fireplace, glancing up into it each time he passed by. "We have to get going. There are a ton of kids who need their presents."

Chris raised an eyebrow at Jared, but he didn't comment. Instead, he gave Sophie a hug and sent her back to bed. Then, he pushed himself to his feet and said, "Sasha, do your magic."

As the kids stepped toward the fireplace, Sasha dusted them again. Within seconds, the small group was back in the sleigh and on their way to the next house.

After Sophie's house, Chris moved faster. Not faster as in running, faster as in he was a blur surrounded by sparkly, yellow magic. At each stop, Sasha stayed in the back, handing Chris the presents. Tracy and Jared tried getting out of the sleigh for the first couple of houses, but by the time their feet touched the roof, Chris was back and ready to go again. Tracy got the feeling Chris had let them out at Sophie's place for a very specific reason, and she figured it had everything to do with Jared.

Jared now seemed like a different person. Instead of the sad, lonely look he had earlier, his eyes danced with excitement. He helped Sasha with the presents. He asked Chris if he could control the reins. (Chris let him.) He helped Chris navigate between the houses. Jared did everything he could to help speed the ride along, because the sun would soon be rising, and they had to be done before then.

After a dozen or so houses, Tracy scooted over so she was sitting next to Jared.

"Are you okay?" she asked him again.

"Yeah," he said with an honest smile. "It's Christmas, and I have a present waiting for me at home."

He didn't sound like he was talking about a new Xbox or an iPad. The word "present" had a stronger, more personal meaning. Tracy wanted to ask what he meant, but she decided not to. If he wanted her to know, he'd tell her. They did exchange phone numbers though, so they could keep in touch. They were on an adventure with the one true Santa Claus. Who else could they talk to about it, except each other?

Santa's bag never seemed to empty. Each time Sasha took presents out, yellow sparkles surrounded the bag. Tracy guessed it was somehow linked to the loading dock back in Alabama and asked Chris why the other Santas had to reload if they could simply use magic.

"Because the other Santas only have Inkling magic. That's not enough to keep the bag full."

"But couldn't you give them some of the magic from your box?"

"Oh, look!" He pointed to the end of a cul de sac. "Our next stop."

On and on they went, until the horizon began to lighten. The sun wasn't up yet, but it soon would be. Tracy was wondering if they would ever finish when Chris steered the reindeer to a sharp left and brought the sleigh down softly on a two-story lime green house.

"Last house," Chris said. "Want to come with me?"

Tracy didn't want to go. She had been inside that particular house a million times. In fact, she had been in the house just a couple of days before, promising Pim that she would find Santa and get help. She had done the first part, but not the second, and she felt sick about it. It didn't matter that Pim would get her presents. Her cousin wouldn't get the present she needed most of all.

CHAPTER FORTY-TWO

Tracy

Tracy took the packages from Sasha and numbly followed Chris out of the sleigh. The lump in her throat kept her from talking.

Tracy had failed. Science fair judges didn't accept "magic" as the result of a science experiment. True, she had a few pictures from her stolen camera, but they weren't enough. And even if they were, she didn't have the right to expose everything Santa Command worked to keep hidden. What would happen if she did? Would they keep doing it once everyone knew the truth? Or would Santa Claus just go away, because people had nothing to believe in? Tracy wouldn't take that risk. She set her pile of presents down and walked to the edge of the roof.

There was a lake in Pim's backyard. It was small, with a few ducks and turtles, and it wasn't too far away. Tracy pulled the camera out of her pocket and hurled it all the way out to the center of the lake. It sunk straight to the bottom.

"What was that?" Chris asked over her shoulder.

"Nothing," Tracy said. "Nothing at all."

She couldn't meet Chris' eyes as she grabbed her presents and walked back to the chimney. "Dust me, Sasha," she said to the Inkling, and she jumped.

Once in the living room, Tracy dropped the presents under the tree and shuffled down the hall to her cousin's first floor bedroom. Pim used to be on the second floor, but since the accident put her in a wheelchair, her parents switched bedrooms with her to make it easier to get around.

Tracy sunk to her knees beside Pim's bed, dropped her forehead onto the mattress, and cried. She didn't hear the footsteps behind her until Chris spoke up.

"Your cousin?"

"Please," Tracy begged. "You have magic. Please fix her."

"Tracy..."

"Please." Tracy looked back at him. "If you heal Pim, I won't ask for another Christmas present ever again. And I promise to always listen to my parents, and clean my room, and—"

"I wish I could." Chris moved up beside her and placed a warm hand on her shoulder. He sounded very sad. "Even I don't have enough magic to undo this."

In her heart, Tracy knew that was the truth. Chris knew when kids were sleeping, and when they were awake, and when they were injured. If he had the power, he would have already fixed her. Hearing him say "no" still ripped her insides to shreds.

Sasha scrambled up onto the bed and gently touched Tracy's arm. "I'm so sorry."

Tracy's eyes burned as the tears came flowing out.

Her sobs were enough to wake Pim. The girl yawned, then blinked a few times, and for a brief second, her eyes focused on the Inkling. Then, she scrunched up her face and squeaked out two words in a completely terrified voice.

"Santa! No!"

CHAPTER FORTY-THREE

Santa Command—Control Room 8
December 25th
0524 hours

Phil clutched the edge of his chair to keep from falling out of it. Paige Murphy's face was there on the view screen, larger than life. Two years had passed since he'd given the order to wipe her memory, but he had never forgotten the horrified look in her eyes right before it happened. She wore that same look now as Tracy knelt next to her bed with tears in her eyes. Sasha was perched on Tracy's shoulder, and Chris and Jared were hovering just inside the door.

What are they doing in there?

Tracy's lips moved, but the camera was in a tree outside the closed window. Phil couldn't hear a word. He spoke into his headset. "Sasha, do you copy?"

The Inkling looked straight at the camera and nodded.

"Good," Phil said. "Get me some audio." It wasn't an order. It was a plea. He needed to hear what was being said in that room.

Sasha fiddled with something on her earpiece. The speakers in Santa Command crackled, then Tracy's voice filled the air.

"—couldn't do it. I screwed up. Big time."

Paige lay on the bed, twisting her head from side to side like she was saying, "no."

"It's okay." Tracy took Paige's hand. "The doctor said the operation will work. We'll find another way to get the money, and we'll fix you. I promise."

Money? Phil leaned forward in his seat. *There's an operation that can fix her?*

Paige's movements grew more frantic. She started whimpering.

Sasha jumped off of Tracy's shoulder and onto the bed. "It's okay, honey." She touched Paige's arm.

Paige opened her mouth wide.

The sounds that she made came out as a cross between a hiss and a gurgle, but there was no mistaking what she said. "Dust! No!" She yanked her hand from Tracy's, balled up her fist, and knocked Sasha across the room.

Sasha yelped. The microphone in her earpiece filled the control room with a deafening squeal.

Everyone but Phil covered their ears. He spoke

urgently into his headset. "Sasha. Sasha, answer me."

"I will as soon as my ears stop ringing." She picked herself up off the carpet and shook her head clear. "That was completely uncalled for."

"No," Phil said, "it wasn't. You're the reason she's like this."

Sasha placed her hands on her hips. "I most certainly am not."

"Well, not you exactly. It was me, but..." Phil's thoughts were too jumbled to say what he needed. If there truly was an operation that could help Paige, he had to talk to Tracy. "It doesn't matter. I have an idea, but I need you all back at Santa Command, now."

CHAPTER FORTY-FOUR

Tracy

Tracy, Jared, Phil, Beth, Walt, Sasha, and Chris were all in the dressing room where they'd put Tracy when she'd first arrived at Santa Command. They were all seated on the couch or on the floor except for Phil, who was pacing the room. He would mumble a couple of words, then stop and start pacing again. Tracy watched him go back and forth like a tennis ball until she couldn't take it anymore.

"Stop," she said. "What are you trying to tell us?" All of the presents had been delivered on time, despite everything Tracy had done. The fake Santas had been deprogrammed and sent home with no memories of their trip. It was Christmas morning, and some kids were already up, squealing for joy at the presents Santa left them. Why was Phil so upset?

Phil stopped and knelt on the floor in front of

Tracy. He may have looked fairly young, but the pain in his eyes made him seem a whole lot older.

"Paige Murphy," he said urgently. "Do you know her?"

"She's my cousin." Tracy didn't know why Phil was asking, but it made her very nervous. Why would he care about her cousin?

"And you said there's an operation that can fix her mind?"

Tracy nodded. Had Chris told them about her plan? Was she in trouble? That thought sent her apology tumbling out. They were just words, but it was all she had. "I'm sorry. I didn't mean to break anything. I just wanted to help her so badly. I thought everything was fixed."

"No," Phil said. "Everything isn't fixed. But I can fix it."

Beth slid off of the couch and knelt by Phil. She touched his shoulder, and that seemed to calm him. "What are you saying?"

"I have money. I've been saving up for a vacation, but you can have it all. Just tell me how much you need."

Tracy pulled her hands out of his. "Why would you do that?"

"Because..." Phil took a deep breath before he let out the words he couldn't say earlier. "I was the one who ordered Paige to be dusted. She sneaked out to spy on Santa, and my job is to prevent that at all costs. You know about our Santas. You know what would happen if we let children see them."

Again Tracy nodded. She didn't fully understand what he was telling her, but she felt sick to her stomach.

Phil continued. "So I had the Inklings alter her memory. I promise you, I didn't know the affect it would have."

"But…but Pim fell out of a tree," Tracy insisted. "That's what happened. She hit her head on the way down."

"*After* I had her dusted."

"No," Tracy said, but she believed him anyway. Pim had been injured because of the person kneeling before her. She buried her face in her hands and started sobbing. Beth pulled her against her shoulder and ran her fingers through Tracy's hair. Beth didn't say anything though. Nothing she could say would bring back the years Pim had lost.

"Wait a second." Chris spoke up for the first time since entering the room. His voice was gravely, like he was exhausted. Tracy couldn't blame him. She felt like she was ready to collapse. "Are you saying Inkling dust made that child the way she is?"

Phil hung his head like he was ready for it to be chopped off.

"You know that's impossible, right? My magic cannot be used to harm children. Even if you tried, it wouldn't work. You may have erased a few seconds of her memory, but you can't take the blame for her brain injury. That, she did when she fell."

Phil looked up. The tiniest bit of light appeared in his eyes. "You mean it's not my fault?"

"No, sir," Chris huffed. "Do you honestly think I'd allow harm to come to a child on my watch?"

"I didn't do it," Phil said softly, just to confirm what Chris said. Then louder, he said, "It's not my fault!"

"Congratulations," Tracy snapped. "You know it doesn't change anything, right?" She knew she sounded rude, but she couldn't help it. Even though the sun was up, the night was still pressing down on her. There was nothing anyone could do. She only wanted to curl up in her bed and sleep for the next three days. She didn't even care about presents.

Phil lifted her chin so their eyes met. "Did you forget? I said I would pay for her operation."

Tracy shook her head. "Weren't you just shouting it wasn't your fault? You don't have to anymore."

"But I want to." He was no longer sad. In fact, it was the first time all night that he had been excited about something. "I joined Santa Command so I could make magic, and this is the most magical thing I can imagine doing. Please, let me do this."

"But how? I can't take a check from a stranger home to my parents."

Beth had an idea. "He could make it anonymous."

"That might work," Phil said. "I'll include a note saying I heard about her operation from a friend, and I wanted to make sure she got it."

"You'll really do this?" Tracy couldn't believe that she had gotten what she came for. It just didn't happen in the way she expected.

"Just let me know where to send the check."

"Thank you." Tracy threw her arms around Phil's neck, knocking him to the ground. The two of them laughed hysterically for the first time in a very long time.

"Wait," Tracy said after their laughter had settled down. "Are you still in trouble?" There was one guy sitting on the couch that she didn't recognize. Was he the boss? If so, she was ready to do some big time groveling. Phil was going to fix her cousin. The least she could do was make sure he kept his job.

Everyone stared at the guy on the couch, who in turn, stared back. "What do you expect me to do? I can't let something like tonight happen again."

Chris cleared his throat, and everyone turned to him. "I'm pretty sure I'm the boss, and I say Phil has a job for as long as he wants it. He brought you here, Tracy, because he was afraid for your health. He stopped time because he was protecting children. He's giving up on his dream for a little girl he doesn't even know. He's exactly the type of person I want working for me."

Walt couldn't argue with that, so he simply said, "Glad you're still on board, Phil."

Everyone in the room cheered while Tracy hugged Phil again.

"Well, I'm glad we were able to work everything out," said Chris while he pushed himself off of the couch. "If you'll excuse me, I have a wife waiting for me at..." His voice faded out, and his body started to shake. He reached for the couch arm, but not soon enough. He collapsed to the floor.

CHAPTER FORTY-FIVE

Santa Command—Dressing Room
December 25th
0546 hours

Phil was the first one by Chris' side. The old guy was still in his Santa suit. That should have been the first clue that something was wrong. Chris would have changed back to his normal clothes the moment he got to Santa Command if he had the magic. But he didn't. The night had taken it all out of him.

Tracy knelt next to Phil. "What happened? What's wrong?"

Jared knelt on his other side. "He's still breathing. That's good, right?"

"Yeah," said Phil. "That's good. But he needs magic. He's centuries old. He can't survive without it."

"Is that why he doesn't deliver presents anymore?" Tracy asked. "Because it's too hard?"

Beth nodded. "When the world became too big, the job became too much. His magic is limited, and over the years, he's used a lot of it up. He has enough to keep both him and Mary alive, but as you can see, even an hour of deliveries weakens him."

"So he created Santa Command?"

"Several hundred stations worldwide. It's far from perfect," Beth shared a look with Phil that said they both agreed, "but he couldn't stand for kids not to get what they needed."

Sasha climbed onto Chris' chest and placed her tiny hand over his heart. "We need to get him home. Back to his magic box."

Phil looked to Tracy and Jared. "You two ready to go through the portal again?"

CHAPTER FORTY-SIX

Jared

Magic existed in the world. It was all around him, and it was important. And now, it was going to save Chris' life.

Jared and Tracy carried Chris through the portal on an improvised stretcher made from Santa coats. Mary met them on the other side and helped them lay Chris down in the center of the library. Phil had contacted Mary already, and the magic box was waiting for them in the room.

Chris seemed so small and fragile lying there on the floor. His cheeks were sunken in. His skin was white and thin as paper. It was even worse that he was still in his Santa outfit and not in his normal clothes.

Jared had no idea what to do. He looked to Mary and said, "Well?"

Mary opened the lid. "How about you do it?"

Inside the box was a brilliant galaxy of stars, leaping and dancing together. It was so bright, it hurt his eyes to look at it, yet he couldn't look away. He knelt beside the box and scooped up a handful of the magic. He smiled at the way it tingled. Everything about it was real. He accepted that now.

"Your turn," Mary said to Tracy.

Tracy knelt next to Jared. She hesitated, and he nodded, encouraging her. She scooped up her own handful, and the two of them carried the magic over to Chris.

"Now what?" Jared asked.

Mary stood behind them and put her hands on their shoulders. "You know what to do."

Together, Jared and Tracy opened their hands and let the magic spill onto Chris' body. A thousand yellow stars dipped and swirled across his chest, around his head, and down to his toes. As the magic did its work, Chris' body transformed. His cheeks filled out and regained their rosy color, his beard disappeared and was replaced by a warm smile, and finally, his eyes opened.

He blinked a few times, then Mary helped him to his feet. A few seconds later, he was back in his navy blue suit and looked just like he had the day Jared met him.

Tracy and Jared hovered around him, unsure of

what to do. A moment before, he had seemed so fragile.

"Come here, you two." Chris opened his arms, and the two children ran into them. "Is there anything I can do for you to thank you for your help?"

Jared didn't know how he had helped, but there was only one thing he wanted anyway. "I'd like to go home."

"Me too," said Tracy.

***

Jared and Beth walked through the door of their apartment. Beth made it about two steps before she collapsed on the couch, but Jared wasn't ready for sleep yet.

He went to his bedroom closet and dug through the pile of dirty clothes. Beneath his favorite pair of jeans, he found the CD. He'd buried it at the bottom of his closet when Chris had given it to him. At the time, Jared thought Chris was just trying to remind him of his dad's favorite band, but after seeing Sophie unwrap the book, Jared knew the present wasn't from Chris. It was from his dad. Just as he suspected, on the inside was a note written on a yellow Post-It.

Jared, Every time I listen to this CD I think of you. I hope you'll listen to it and think of me. Love, Dad

Jared clutched the CD to his chest. Maybe it was time to think of his dad again. Of both of his parents.

He put the CD in his player, set it to repeat, and crawled into bed, listening as the music crept into his dreams.

CHAPTER FORTY-SEVEN

Tracy

Sasha offered to take Tracy home. Their first stop was Pim's house. It was barely after 6 am, and no one was up yet. Tracy was glad for that, because she wasn't there to talk to anyone. Sasha popped the two of them into the living room, and Tracy pulled a plain white envelope out of her pocket. She placed it on one of the lower branches of the Christmas tree, making sure the words "For Pim" were facing out, and smiled.

Her next stop was home, more specifically, her bed. Her parents would expect her to wake up soon, and she was certain she'd hear her mother screaming happily when the call came from Pim's parents telling them about the envelope. But for now, Tracy wanted to lie in bed and remember the night.

It had been magical. Not just because of the actual magic, but because of everything she'd seen and done.

She wanted to relive every detail before she forgot it. She even wondered if she could do it again next year, minus the breaking things.

"Here," Sasha reached into one of her bags.

For a second, Tracy thought about ducking under her covers. Were they going to wipe her memory after all?

But Sasha didn't pull out a handful of dust. It was Tracy's phone. "Phil asked me to give this to you."

It was in perfect shape, not a scratch on it, but Tracy had the feeling a few pictures had been deleted from it. She placed it on her night stand and snuggled under her comforter. "Thanks. It's been a crazy night, hasn't it?"

"What makes you say that?"

Tracy ticked a list off on her fingers. "Well, there was the computer, and Chris, and the million different Santas."

Sasha laughed so loud that Tracy thought her parents might hear her and wake up. But they didn't. Sasha placed her hand on Tracy's arm. "Oh, honey. You think Santa Command is crazy? You should see Tooth Fairy Central. Now that place will blow your mind."

Tracy smiled, but kept her mouth shut, because an idea was forming in her head. Maybe she wouldn't have to wait a year for another adventure. She stuck her tongue on one of her molars and wiggled it. In a few days, it would be loose enough to pull.

ACKNOWLEDGEMENTS

This book would not exist if it weren't for my critique partner, Dianne K. Salerni. She encouraged me to keep going when I thought it was pointless. I also need to thank her for saying, "I'd really like to meet Beth's son." Confession time—Jared wasn't even a spark of an idea until she asked to meet him. Thank you, also, to Amy Christine Parker and Jennifer Baker for your invaluable insight.

I am, of course, very grateful to my husband who understands that I must escape to the bookstore on Saturday mornings. My productivity increases ten-fold when I have my quiet table and my chocolate caramel mocha.

I'd also like to thank everyone at Month9Books for believing in my story and for loving Tracy, Jared, and Phil as much as I do. You are all rock stars and helped me to bring out the best parts of this book.

And thank you to everyone who believes in the magic of Santa Claus.

KRYSTALYN DROWN

Krystalyn spent thirteen years working at Walt Disney World in a variety of roles: entertainer, talent coordinator, and character captain. Her degree in theatre as well as many, many hours spent in a dance studio, helped with her job there. Her various other day jobs have included working in zoology at Sea World, as an elementary teacher, and currently as a support technician for a website. In the evenings, she does mad writing challenges with her sister, who is also an author. Krystalyn lives near Orlando, Florida with her husband, son, a were cat, and a Yorkie with a Napoleon complex.

*Preview more great middle grade titles from
Tantrum Books*

Visit www.month9books.com/tantrumbooks